Threads of Blue

Threads of Blue

SUZANNE LaFLEUR

WENDY
LAMB
BOOKS

Text copyright © 2017 by Suzanne M. LaFleur
Jacket and map art copyright © 2017 by Jensine Eckwall

All rights reserved. Published in the United States by
Wendy Lamb Books, an imprint of Random House Children's Books,
a division of Penguin Random House LLC, New York.

Wendy Lamb Books and the colophon are trademarks of
Penguin Random House LLC.

Visit us on the Web! randomhousekids.com

Educators and librarians, for a variety of teaching tools,
visit us at RHTeachersLibrarians.com

Library of Congress Cataloging-in-Publication Data
Names: LaFleur, Suzanne M., author.
Title: Threads of blue / Suzanne LaFleur.
Description: First edition. | New York : Wendy Lamb Books, [2017] | Sequel to:
Beautiful blue world. | Summary: Mathilde escapes war-torn Sofarende and reunites
with Megs and the other children who are working for the army to retake Sofarende
from the enemy, but Mathilde must come to terms with her past treasonous actions
and determine what she must do in order to prove her friendship to Megs.
Identifiers: LCCN 2016048219 (print) | LCCN 2017023491 (ebook) |
ISBN 978-1-101-94001-3 (eBook) | ISBN 978-1-101-93999-4 (trade) |
ISBN 978-1-101-94000-6 (lib. bdg.) | ISBN 978-1-101-94002-0 (pbk.)
Subjects: | CYAC: War—Fiction. | Espionage—Fiction. | Friendship—Fiction.
Classification: LCC PZ7.L1422 (ebook) | LCC PZ7.L1422 Thr 2017 (print) |
DDC [Fic]—dc23

The text of this book is set in 11.95-point Caslon.
Interior design by Heather Kelly

Printed in the United States of America
10 9 8 7 6 5 4 3 2 1
First Edition

For Elizabeth,

agent extraordinaire

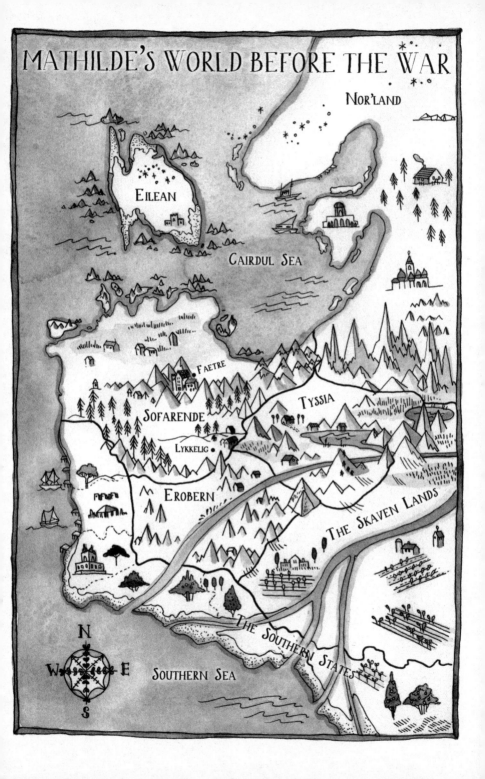

THE KINGDOM OF EILEAN,

in Partnership with the Republic of Sofarende,

decrees that

MATHILDE JOSS

be provided with immediate transport and entry into Eilean for essential war work.

D. Rohbears, of Eilean

E. Markusen, of Sofarende

1

THE SKY STRETCHED ABOVE me, pale with streaks of pink.

Beautiful.

But where was our ceiling? Had my house been blown open in the night?

Or was I dead, and this was what was next? Did our souls really rise up when our bodies went into the ground? To sway in the sky?

Because my bed lifted and sank, lifted and sank.

I must be sick.

Why didn't Mother come to feel my forehead, to check my fever, to cool me?

My sisters cried, sharp and piercing. Poor Kammi and Tye must have been sick, too.

Where was Mother? Father? Didn't they hear us? Why didn't they come?

"I'll help you," I tried to tell Kammi and Tye. I reached out my hand from under the blankets.

No, one wasn't a blanket, it was my coat. That was right,

it had been a bombing night. I'd slept under my coat. The other *was* a blanket, but not my own. It was gray-blue, woolen, heavy, and damp. It smelled fishy, like the sea.

The sea, the sea . . .

The sea . . .

The sea!

Gulls cried above us.

Not my sisters.

The boat's motors slowed.

Land ahead.

"Are you feeling better?" the fisherman asked.

Had I been sick, then? "Better?"

"Rough night. After it got choppy you lay down, clutching your stomach."

It *was* better knowing that Mother wasn't here. Better than having called and called her when I was sick, to have her ignore me and Kammi and Tye, when we needed her. She wouldn't do that.

"I feel okay. That's Eilean?"

"It is."

My stomach gave another awful swoop.

I had never been to Eilean. I would set foot in a new country for the first time.

Alone.

But Megs, my best friend, would be there. She had set out ahead of me. We would find each other. She had said she would be with me, whatever happened. I was the one who'd fallen behind, but I'd promised to catch up.

Megs?

Megs?

I called for her in my heart, like we'd practiced.

4

It had worked one time in the past, our silent way of reaching for each other.

But there was no answer.

My fault.

I sat up. I felt better looking over the edge of the boat—watching the deep blue water rock and sway made it feel more natural for my body to be doing it, too.

"What are you meant to do in Eilean?" the fisherman asked.

I watched the waves for another moment, gently biting my lip.

"I don't know. I was just told to get there."

I was sorry I couldn't tell him more. He had shuttled me across the water overnight at a moment's notice. Could I say that the Tyssia-Erobern Empire was about to occupy Sofarende?

I knew that our country was far behind us, but its absence from the horizon made a lump rise in my throat.

As if Sofarende already were no more.

I might not be welcome back there anyway, not ever again, if anyone had figured out what I'd done.

"You should stay when we get to Eilean," I said, the most I could hint.

"I've got two little ones at home. They're probably worried because I didn't come back last night."

A boy and a girl, faces pressed against their front window, waiting for their father. Their mother, even more anxious, pretending she wasn't, hovering nearby.

I sat back and drew my knees up to my chest.

"I'm sorry. It's my fault you didn't go home." We should have taken the time to get his family. I hadn't thought.

"Not at all. Orders are orders."

"How did you stay out of the military?" I asked. Most men his age had been called up to serve.

"Twisted leg. My foot turns the wrong way. No good for marching. But just fine in a boat. My arms are strong, I can cast out my net and pull it back in. . . . How did you get in it?"

"Didn't they have the test in your town?"

"What test?"

Maybe they hadn't. Or maybe he hadn't paid attention because his own children were too young. "The Army Adolescent Aptitude Test. For children who wanted to serve." If you'd passed the test, you had to spend the rest of the war in the army. But they'd taken us from the bombed cities, kept us safe and fed. It was what my parents had hoped for.

"What are you, twelve years old?"

"Almost thirteen." I tightened my arms around my knees, pulling them to my chest.

"What is the world coming to?"

Did anyone know?

I raised my eyes to the sky. Still no aerials.

"Are there dybnauts out here?" On land, I feared attack from the sky; on the sea, should I look into the depths below, for the deep-undersea boats? The public believed that Tyssia had no access to the sea, but at Faetre, the manor house full of war secrets where we who'd passed the test had worked, my friend Annevi had told me otherwise.

"In the night I saw plenty of Sofarender and Eilean ships headed in the same direction as us. All sizes. What's going on?"

I bit my lip again. "You should pick up your children and come back."

"I don't have permits to land in Eilean."

"Wait—you—?"

"Calm down. You do. Your yellow transit card is pretty powerful."

"But if you can't land—"

"You'll swim."

"Swim! I—I can't!"

"A Sofarender who can't swim?"

"I'm from the south, not the coast—I—"

"They didn't teach you that in your training?"

"I didn't have any kind of training."

Unfortunately.

The fisherman shook his head in amused disbelief. *First they take children into the army, then they provide them with no training whatsoever.*

I had no good answers for him. It had seemed like our proctors had cared for us. Had maybe saved our lives by taking us.

Now that it was lighter out, I could see that the fisherman's stubble had grown in overnight. His wife was probably looking over his razor and other shaving things. *Doesn't he need them? Will he ever come back to use them?*

There was still time for them to be reunited before Tyssia got to the northern port towns, wasn't there?

"Don't worry," the fisherman said. "I'll send you with a buoy."

He didn't mean don't worry about his family. He meant don't worry about him pitching me into the sea.

"Won't my card allow you to dock the boat just to let me out?"

"Going to let you out near a beach. I've headed farther west to get away from the other ships and boats. I don't know about any docks. I'll cut the engines entirely as we get into shallow water."

"I can't get all wet."

"Of course you can get wet."

"No, it's not me, it's . . ."

I drew my coat closer. The fisherman studied its thick bulk. Too thick for the season, too padded for the wartime scarcity of fabric. Stuffed full of the documents I'd been asked to bring.

"Heaven above." He raised his eyes up. Then he looked back down at me. "Whatever you've got on you, it will dry out. And if not, I was under the impression that the most important thing was to get your feet on that damp Eilean soil, isn't it?"

That, I was not sure of. Not anymore.

I stared out at the water, at Eilean's coast growing as we neared. The shoreline alternated between cliffs and short beaches.

We were more to the Examiner and her team than just transporters, weren't we? She had picked us for our minds. She cared about us as people.

Didn't she?

The fisherman cut the engines, leaving us bobbing several hundred yards from the sand.

A peaceful, quiet, empty place.

How could there be such a war?

The fisherman stood and came over to me, arms out-stretched to help me put my coat back on, the way I imagined he helped his children into their coats when it was time for school.

Father had always helped us into our coats like that, too.

The lump returned to my throat.

"Button up good," the fisherman instructed. As I did, he removed his belt, looped it around my middle, and cinched it tight.

"That should keep the whatever-it-is in place."

"Thanks."

Then he handed me what looked like a large pretend pastry, but it was hard.

"What is this?"

"It floats. Hug it tight to your chest. There, like that." He looped a rope through the hole in its center, double- and triple-knotted it. The rope looked thin, but I hoped it was strong.

I took a deep breath, looking over my shoulder at the water.

"I'll pull you back in if things look bad. Face the shore at a diagonal, kick, and you can maybe ride in on the waves if the pull is right."

The extent of my swimming lesson.

He gave me a big smile.

I tried to smile back, but my stomach churned like the choppy water.

"Good luck, Mathilde."

"Thank you," I said, as sincerely as I could. "I'll never forget what you did for me." *I hope you get back to your family.*

Were there Tyssian dybnauts, waiting to get him on the way back?

Waiting for me?

I looked over the side of the boat.

Cold! Cold! Cold!

I drew in my breath. My mouth flooded with the icy sea. *Salt!*

I struggled to get my head above the water. Choking, my body remembered the instructions: my arms held tight to the floating pastry; my legs kicked.

I broke the surface. The fisherman yelled, "That's it! That's it!" My head didn't go back under again.

My eyes stung, but I fixed them on Eilean and kicked and kicked.

When I relaxed, the water lifted me, up and down, up and down, as it had lifted the boat.

And that was how I was borne by the sea onto the shore of Eilean.

I landed, flat on my stomach, face in the sand. I spat and blinked.

I tried to catch my breath as the pastry bobbed all the way back to the fisherman. When it reached him, he wound the rope up around it.

My cord to Sofarende was cut.

I could not go back.

And probably shouldn't, as the last thing I'd done before I left was commit treason.

The fisherman raised his hand in a long, still wave. I

stood and raised mine, held it high, so he could see me wave back, so that he would know I was all right, that he had succeeded, though my arms were shaking from gripping the pastry so tight.

Would he make it back to Sofarende?

Would it still be there?

Were there dybnauts lurking, making the way back dangerous?

Please let him be safe on the way back. Please don't let anything happen to him because he helped me.

I had done it. I had made it to Eilean.

I plopped back down onto the sand, breathing hard.

I looked up and down the beach.

Disappointment rippled through me.

Megs wasn't there, waving in welcome.

No one was on the beach at all.

I stood and peeled off layer after layer of wet clothing until I was standing in my underthings. I spread out the nightclothes I hadn't taken off in days. I reached into my coat's inside pocket. The landing card and IDs were okay— wet, but readable. The sopping clump of papers ... how much trouble would I be in for ruining them? Documents so precious, they would use a child to smuggle them across international borders during wartime.

The text was typed and had survived the water, but the words looked like gibberish. Coded. Or cyphered. Smart. Caelyn or Brid could have started marking them for patterns, but they probably couldn't have read them, even though coded, typed pages were their specialty at Faetre. Maybe Tommy or Hamlin could. They were geniuses.

I set the papers out to dry, weighing each down with rocks.

They would be a crinkly, sandy mess.

When she saw them, the Examiner would say, "Did you *swim* to Eilean?"

And I would say yes.

The wind tugged at the papers, trying to set them free.

If I lost them . . .

One got loose. I hurried after it, shouting, "Wait!"

Not that the page could hear me.

I caught up with it, panting.

Holding the paper tightly, I took in which one it was.

Not a secret document.

Something more precious.

My sisters' handprints.

Little Tye's. And Kammi's. With mine.

The paint had held up well. The water hadn't ruined the images.

I sat down, holding the paper tightly as the wind threatened to whisk it from my grasp.

I took the risk of letting go on one side to press my right hand over my own right handprint.

My hand was slightly bigger than the print.

I had grown.

It had only been a few months, but I had grown.

Had they grown, too?

My stomach clenched.

Already, their hands wouldn't match the ones on this paper. Their hair would be longer. Tye's baby-plump cheeks would be thinner.

But I hoped so. Of course I did. Even if it meant we would one day meet each other and feel like strangers, I wanted them to grow.

Because if they weren't growing . . .

Where were they? Still at home? Still with Mother and Father? Had our family been torn apart even further since my parents had sent me to Faetre?

Did they know the danger that every Sofarender was in?

Were they hurt or scared?

I weighed the paper down.

And then I took both my hands and pressed them firmly into the sand, making my mark on this land.

2

I WOKE AGAIN TO a stretch of sky, this time of hazy sunshine.

The sea broke on the shore nearby, no longer rocking me. My stomach was less queasy, but it grumbled.

I sat up.

I felt damp, though not quite as cold, except for my toes, icy in the moist sand. Did they look a bit purple? I rubbed each foot quickly with my hands.

My clothes would never dry on the beach. I pulled on my nightgown, my socks. My shoes squished when I shoved in my feet.

The papers were no longer soaked, but they were still droopy. They wouldn't be able to dry properly, either. I freed them from under the rocks and collected them in a stack, and carefully folded up my sisters' handprints. Then I sat, studying another page covered in paint.

All blue paint.

Rainer's picture of the things that made him happiest. Of home. When it had been his home. The picture that showed both of us what the world could be when it was perfect, when people cared about each other, whoever they were. The picture—the vision—he had entrusted to me when I'd helped him escape.

Even though he was Tyssian.

Where *was* Rainer?

He hadn't had a card to get transport to Eilean like I had. And if the Tyssians had found him, after he had been our prisoner . . .

The swollen papers made a fatter stack than they had before. I wasn't sure if they'd fit back in my coat; if they did, I would have a huge middle.

I decided just to carry the coat over my arm, buttoned and belted shut.

I looked around.

I was still alone.

What was I supposed to do?

A steep path led off the beach.

Steep, but walkable.

I climbed up the dunes and let myself turn around. Was that Sofarende, across the water, or an illusion in the haze?

I came over the top of the hill.

Soldiers. Trucks of rolled barbed wire, poles for pilings.

I froze.

"Go home, little girl," said the man in charge as the others descended the path to the beach with their supplies.

"What are you doing?" I asked in Eilian. What did my accent sound like to him?

"Protecting the beaches. Don't want the Tyssians to land."

Did that mean they had taken all of Sofarende, way up north to the sea now?

The man saw my stricken face, tried to give me a smile. "Don't you worry. Run along home."

If he had heard the accent on my tongue, he didn't seem to be bothered by it. Maybe because I was so young, and a girl.

Should I take out my identification, show him? Could he help me figure out where to go? I had imagined presenting myself to people behind a desk, that was the sort of military work I was used to, but these men on the beach—what would they think of my Sofarender military status? Of how I had just washed up on the shore they were about to protect?

My stomach turned. If I had been an hour or two later, the beach could have been covered in barbed wire. The waves could have crashed me right into it. I would have been tangled and cut and choking, all at once.

"You live around here?" he asked, when I hadn't budged.

"My uncle—over there." The lie slipped out easily. I gestured in the direction of the only house in sight, way off along the cliffs. If he *was* thinking about my Sofarender accent, it might make sense to him, with all that was going on, for Sofarender parents to send their daughters to relatives in Eilean, if they were lucky enough to have any.

He didn't seem to doubt me. "Don't go wandering now. Go home."

I headed toward the house.

Maybe there was food there.

I walked the coastal road, but the house looked farther and farther away.

My feet dragged. The salty air touched heavy on my tongue. My lips were getting chapped, my forehead sunburned.

More truckloads of soldiers and barricading supplies passed.

None paid any attention to me.

Which was foolish.

I was an undeclared foreigner.

In wartime.

What did they know?

I looked up at the sky.

Still no aerials.

But soon?

If Sofarende *had* fallen, Tyssia could have aerfields just miles away.

I could hear them.

I looked up again.

The house blinked in and out of sight like a bad light.

I squinted.

It was there, wasn't it?

I was headed toward *something*. Wasn't I?

The wind whipped past, the salt stinging my eyes and face, making my loose, unusually fuzzy hair stick in my eyes and mouth, but for some reason, I couldn't lift my hand to draw it away.

The whipping wind shifted everything.

My usual nightmare.

The nightmares that were not just nightmares.

Built on memories.

Memories that were not only mine. Rainer's, too.

My loved ones flickered before me.

Father, with his post office cap and clean uniform.

What was he doing in Eilean?

Mother and Tye and Kammi, too.

They must have gotten word in time, gotten on a boat just before I did!

I saw them, but couldn't reach them. I couldn't catch them.

That was how the nightmares worked.

Oh, but there was Megs! She *had* been bound for Eilean, like me, with the Examiner, who had taken care of us at Faetre. Megs and the other children would have made it ahead of me, she was waiting for me, looking for me. With dark braids like she had always had back home—no, she had short hair, like they'd cut all our hair at Faetre. She stretched her hand out to me.

I lifted my hand, but again, I reached nothing.

My family and my dear friend vanished.

Megs?

I thought her name into the wind. I tried to call her again from my heart.

Megs? I'm sorry I let us get separated. Are you here?

It was only when I lowered my hand that I realized the whipping wind had stopped, blocked by the house in front of me.

The house.

But it was hard to focus on, what with the red splotches.

They swam before me until they settled into three distinct shapes.

Poppies, nailed to the doorframe.

Tipping and swaying like I was in the sea surf again, I lifted my feet to carry me up the steps.

My hand stretched out for the door and did its best to knock.

The door was flung open by a girl younger than me.

Not Kammi.

Not Tye.

Not Megs.

A stranger.

I tried to explain myself, to ask for water.

She shrieked.

"Mummy! Dada! There's a Tyssian girl on the porch!"

My head swam, my stomach full of the churning sea. The water sloshing over my ears, my eyes. A narrowing yellow tunnel. Black splotches reared up, swirling, covering the features of the girl's face.

But this was important.

I needed her to know.

I found the words carefully, in Eilian.

"I am a Sofarender."

The tunnel closed in.

3

"OH GOOD, YOU'RE AWAKE! Dada says you're starving. And you need some water. Here. You'll have to sit up to drink. You're in my bed."

I blinked at the girl. No chance I could sit up yet, not even for water.

She held the glass above me.

I managed to shake my head.

She lowered the glass, looking disappointed.

"Your things are all over there, on the chair. We didn't disturb anything."

I nodded, relieved.

"Dada says you *are* from Sofarende, your identification card in your pocket says so. And that envelope full of money is Sofarender currency. But how did you get here?"

I lifted myself onto my elbows. The tunnel didn't ripple in my sight; it must have gone. I blinked, to make sure.

"I fainted?"

The girl nodded. She tipped the cup against my lips and I took a clumsy sip of water.

"I'm Angelica," she said.

I didn't answer; I didn't have the energy. She probably knew my name already from my identification card.

Mathilde.

Mathilde Joss.

When I seemed steady enough, she handed me the glass, and I took a few more sips.

Then she gave me a thin sandwich of buttered bread from a plate on the nightstand.

I gobbled it up. I looked to see if the girl was smiling, finding my behavior funny.

It seemed she didn't.

There wasn't anything funny about being so hungry.

They knew it here, too, then. Hunger.

Angelica sat carefully on the end of my bed. Her bed. "You should know ... we've been hearing on the radio ... your country ..."

I gazed out the window into the fading light of the now-cloudy sky.

I looked at Angelica, who was struggling to finish her sentence, to tell me this thing she knew would be awful for me to hear.

"I already know."

We went downstairs to the living room, where her parents sat by the radio. These big boxes, for news broadcasts and entertainment, existed in Sofarende, but we hadn't had one. I didn't know any family who had their own. There had been some at Faetre. We'd had everything at Faetre. Maps and telephones and decoder machines.

At first, looking around at the comforts of their living room—the faded pink rug, the painted porcelain figurines, the colorful knitted blankets on the backs of the sofa and chairs—I felt like a stranger. In Sofarende, we hadn't had much that was decorative or extra. I breathed in the fragrance from the bowl of dried flowers on the table; they had even decorated the air.

My heart beat slowly, pounding a heavy rhythm in my neck and wrists and legs. After a while, I couldn't make out the smell of the flowers anymore. The intricate pattern on the rug became as familiar as the maps of Sofarende we'd had all over Faetre. I stopped trying to decide if Angelica's fluffy curls were blond or brown; they just were the same color they'd always been.

The voice on the radio said, "After a two-day attack, representatives from the governments of Sofarende and the Tyssian Empire meet to sign the formal surrender of Sofarende. The Tyssian flag now flies over the whole Continent, and we mourn with our brothers in Sofarende as we prepare for the possibility of attack on our own soil. . . ."

Angelica, beside me, kept looking at me, as if she expected me to fall apart at the loss of my country. As if she didn't know whether I might need someone to hold my hand. As if making sure I was still really there, in their house, proving the news reports that something had gone terribly wrong in my country.

But it was her mother whose face fell and crumpled, who covered her mouth and her eyes in turn, who finally couldn't listen anymore, who left the room.

Angelica's father snapped off the radio.

. . .

Angelica's father made dinner. Her mother joined us at the table for the carrots and cabbage, the thin-shaven meat.

A feast, to me.

I tried to eat slowly, counting to ten as I chewed each bite.

No one spoke. Forks and knives clinked. It was strange to sit down at a table, like a family. Not just because it was with someone else's family, but because it had been months since I had eaten a meal with my own.

Did they always eat in silence? Or was it the terrible news making them so quiet? Their fear that Eilean, sitting across a small sea passage, would be next to fall? Was it fear that had made Angelica's mother cry?

Her food was served in a bowl of broth rather than on a plate like ours. She slowly spooned up the broth and then pushed the bowl with meat and vegetables toward Angelica.

"Can Mathilde live with us now?" Angelica asked.

"I don't think so," her dada said.

"Please? *Please?* I've never had a sister. Mummy?"

Her mother looked down at the table. Her father cleared his throat.

Angelica flushed pink.

Why was it bad to wish for a sister? She shouldn't have been made to feel ashamed.

"Little girls aren't like stray animals, Angelica. We can't just keep them. Girls belong somewhere."

My cheeks grew hot as I quartered a small carrot.

I wasn't sure that I did belong anywhere, anymore.

Even Mother and Father had sent me away.

Angelica glanced between me and her parents.

"Angelica, go upstairs with your mother and run her a bath."

Angelica nodded and her mother followed her upstairs.

I set down my empty glass.

I hadn't been dismissed.

I knew what was coming.

But first, Angelica's father held out his hand. "I'm Mr. Parmeter."

I shook. Waited.

"You're a child, and I'm happy to help you. But you need to be honest with me. What are you doing here?"

My work, my life were mostly secret. That had been a condition of life at Faetre: what we did was to be kept from all outsiders, and even our friends on the inside, sometimes. Which was why almost none of the other kids had known I'd been assigned to talk to Rainer.

But Mr. Parmeter had seen my ID cards; he knew I was in the military and only twelve. That I was caked in salt and sand from climbing out of the sea. That I'd escaped just in time.

"I was part of a group. We were being evacuated to Eilean before Sofarende fell. I got separated from them."

He didn't need to know why I'd been separated.

He didn't need to know about helping Rainer escape.

Nobody did.

"What was your group? I'd believe you were just being evacuated for safety if you didn't have such high military intelligence clearance."

I let my breath out. "Did you look at my papers?"

"No. Of course not. I don't want to interfere with whatever it is you're here to do. We're on the same side, after all. I can't imagine how you're involved. You're only a couple of years older than Angelica. I want to help you get where you need to go—but if you *are* on the wrong side, handing you over would be turning you in, so, right or wrong, that's the only way forward."

"Handing me over?"

"Only the authorities could help you find your group, right?"

I nodded. That was probably true.

"So we'll go there."

"Where?"

"Several miles east, there's a branch handling the influx of refugees from the Continent. There's so many."

I nodded . . . Megs, Gunnar, Annevi, Brid, Caelyn . . . all my friends from Faetre . . . they could all be there.

"You . . . do want to rejoin them?"

"Of course!"

What had he read on my face?

He couldn't know. He *couldn't*.

"I'm sorry, of course you do. You must be overwhelmed. And tired. You can have a bath. And we'll find you something clean to wear. Angelica's things might be too small, but my wife isn't very big, so maybe something of hers will do."

I looked down at my dingy nightclothes. All those clothes that Mother had made sure I had to take to Faetre, some of them new . . . all left behind.

"Would you mind sleeping in Angelica's room? There's

another room, but it would . . . it would just be easiest to put you in together. Is that all right?"

"I . . ." I met his eye. I couldn't even thank him.

"No need . . . in a few days this house could be filled up with soldiers, or refugees, without my having a say in the matter. But as for you, tonight . . . I would hope that someone would be kind to my daughter, if she were in your place."

Back home, when the bombings had started, our very own neighbor had grumbled about giving us shelter.

"Don't cry. We'll find your people. Go on upstairs and get some rest."

4

I WOKE SLOWLY, HAIR brushing my face, curling in the salty air.

The sea, the sea. The salt air by the sea.

I could taste it, its memory fresh.

It tasted like something else that was familiar, but I couldn't place it.

Something that made me think of Mother and Father, and the day I'd left Sofarende, and, for some reason, the day our team at Faetre had helped shoot down Tyssian aerials.

The arms and legs tangled up with mine belonged to a girl I'd only just met. She'd wanted us to be like sisters. It had seemed like the wrong thing to say for more reasons than her father had explained.

But we'd played sisters anyway. She'd drawn me a bath after her mother's and took my dirty clothes away and brought me a clean nightgown that was only slightly too big. We'd whispered in the night as we fell asleep, wondering what was happening across the water.

Sisters, sisters.

Were Kammi and Tye okay? And Megs?

How had the world changed so much in one day that this stranger and I clung to each other?

Sofarenders and Eileans were cousins, way back. We were made of each other. We were friends.

The sea air poured in through the open window. I breathed it down deep, to my core, to feel out the memory of my seafaring ancestors. Ancient Sofarers and Eileans and Nor'landers had crossed back and forth across the Cairdul Sea in friendship, slowly building out the world, the peoples we'd become.

And when I felt almost at peace, at home in this new place, a rock formed in the pit of my stomach:

The Tyssians were also our cousins.

And they were killing us.

Extra clothes waited on a chair across Angelica's room, as well as my own underclothes, cleaned, dried, and folded.

I would have liked to think that it was Angelica's mother who had found the clothes and set them out, who had washed my things and hung them to dry by the stove, but I couldn't imagine her having felt well enough last night. She'd gone to bed before I did. It was probably Angelica's father who'd done it.

I sorted through the worn sweaters, button-up shirts, and knee-length skirts, then dressed slowly, the care of strangers soft against my skin.

Angelica finally woke up.

"You're still here!"

I nodded.

"I wondered if you were a dream."

"No."

She sat up, and then she looked worried.

"If you're real, does that mean that it's also real, that Sofarende fell?"

I nodded again.

She sprang out of bed.

"I'll get dressed, too. Then we can go downstairs and see if there's any news."

I waited for her to pull on a plain flower-print dress, and then she ran ahead of me, skipping steps the way only someone at home can.

Her parents were in the kitchen, her mother sitting in front of a steaming cup of dark tea, her father wearing an apron in front of the stove, a pan of creamy yellow eggs on the burner.

"Sit, girls. Breakfast."

We sat for the eggs and soft brown bread that was almost sweet like cake.

My nightgown hung on a line. It showed my journey, from rips and tatters, and grass and dirt stains, to its still-dingy color, like the sand and sea couldn't be washed out of it.

"What's been going on?" Angelica asked.

"There hasn't been a lot of news beyond what we heard last night. I think communication out of Sofarende has been disrupted. After breakfast, I'm going to take Mathilde on her way."

"Can I come?" Angelica asked.

"I'd rather you stay here with your mother."

Angelica frowned, but looked at her mother and quickly replaced her frown with a blank expression.

I returned my empty plate to Angelica's dada at the sink and went over to my nightgown.

"I think it's ruined," he said.

I unpinned it and took it out on the front porch and sat down, hugging the worn cloth to my knees.

The door opened and footsteps came up next to me. A hand touched my shoulder.

Not Angelica. Her mother.

"You can take the nightgown you wore last night. And some of our clothes." Her voice was soft and tired; I realized it was the first time that I'd heard it. Whatever was making her talk to me now, I owed her a little bit back.

"My mother made this for me," I explained. "It's the last thing I have."

"I see." She took it from me gently, examining it. "If I had more time, I would be able to clean it better, and mend it. Would you like that? If you left it with me, and I fixed it? You could . . . come back for it, one day."

I nodded. Why would she be so nice to me?

"And it's not the only thing you have." She ran her fingers through my hair, threading them deep through the tangles and rubbing my scalp. "*You* are from your mother, so she's always with you."

She turned in the direction of the water, her expression shifting to sadness, as if she could look all day, look and look, and never see what she wanted to see. Her lips pressed together tight, as if to block out that salt taste on the air. "Part of me will always be in Sofarende, though I have never been there."

If I could just remember what that taste reminded me of, maybe we could understand each other better. We both seemed to notice it, to want to be rid of it.

I reached for her hand when she pulled it out of my hair, but I missed. She looked at me once more and then went back inside, taking the nightgown with her.

Angelica came outside with my coat, a change of clothes, the borrowed nightgown, and the documents and money all stowed in a bag. It was too hot for coats now. I wouldn't need one for months. It was hard to think of something months away when I didn't even know what was going to happen that afternoon. When I didn't even know where I was going to sleep that night.

I set the bag on the porch and followed Angelica away from the house. When I turned to look back at it, I saw that the red flowers I might have imagined yesterday were really there, made of paper, nailed onto the front of the house.

"What are the poppies for?" I asked Angelica.

"I had three brothers. All lost in the war already."

I stared at her.

"Defending Sofarende," she added, looking away from me.

I followed her eyes toward the water, where her mummy had been looking earlier.

Her sons had been lost. For nothing. Sofarende had fallen anyway. And maybe Eilean would be next.

It was worse than what had happened to me. I'd been sent away, but at least I could hope that my sisters were still okay. And Mother and Father could hope that I was okay.

An ache settled in my chest.

"I'm sorry," I said.

It wasn't enough.

Angelica looked away. "Want to go out on the bluff? I know Dada, he'll clean up. We have time."

I followed her out to the top of a cliff over the beach below. We weren't so close to the edge, not enough for anything to happen, but I noticed again how Angelica's feet moved differently from mine, knowing already where they wanted to step. The ground was soft and sandy, and my feet were not sure of anything.

I looked out over the water and gasped.

It was just a pale, bumpy strip, a slight change in the blue-green horizon, but it was there all the same.

"Yes, that's Sofarende," Angelica said. "You can see it only sometimes, when the light is just right."

The breeze lifted, as if coming all the way across the water. It played with our hair. It tried to talk to us.

"I used to come out here and just look, thinking that maybe I would see a boat bringing my brothers home."

That was probably what her mother was looking for, too.

And when a boat finally came, all it brought was me.

Angelica looked at me again, studying. Wondering why I was here?

"Come on," she said. "We should go back. Dada might be ready now."

I followed her again.

While we were facing away from the sea, a strange sensation started in my chest, replacing the ache with squeezing fear. It took me a minute to realize it was caused by a familiar sound.

My breath caught. I struggled to remember where I was, because this sound didn't fit. The nightmare colors flashed in my mind. The reds and blacks.

It was like they followed me everywhere. From home to Faetre and on to—

"Angelica—"

Just in front of her house, she turned.

"What?"

But she saw them first, behind me.

Tyssian aerials, marked underneath with tiger stripes, zoomed over us.

Angelica's parents came out of the house.

The four of us watched as the aerials headed over the coastline and turned back toward Sofarende.

After several minutes, Angelica's father said, "Just a little show, girls. To get us frightened. But we won't be, right?"

"That's right, Dada," Angelica said. She took her mother's hand and squeezed it.

My heart was still pounding. Easy for Angelica to say she wasn't frightened. She hadn't seen whole blocks of houses flattened to rubble.

Angelica's dada looked at me. "We'll go soon. I'll be right back."

Her parents went inside, exchanging significant looks.

I picked up my small bag by the handles and trailed out to the car after Angelica.

She turned to face me. "I will never forget having a sister for a day."

"You didn't. Not like you really had brothers."

Angelica paused; then she said, "I know. Not like that. But still, it was nice not to be alone. Even for one day."

I squeezed her hand, but then we were hugging. I knew exactly what she meant.

"Isn't it strange, that my brothers died for your country

and now here you are? You are okay, where it is safe. So maybe it wasn't for nothing."

I loved that she thought that, but it hadn't worked that way at all. And she and I weren't exactly safe—if we were, probably not for long. I knew what followed where Tyssian aerials could reach.

Her brothers really had died for nothing.

Certainly, if she thought they'd died for me, that wasn't worth it.

How did she not hate me?

I looked this lonely, somehow strong girl in the eyes.

I couldn't promise her anything.

Not that we'd live through the war.

Not that Tyssia wouldn't invade her country, too.

Not even that I'd try my best to help, because I didn't know what I could do.

Promises were hard to keep.

So I said, "I'm glad I got to meet you."

And she hugged me tight again.

Angelica's dada came back out and told her to stay in the house. She waved to me as I climbed into the open car and her father shut the door.

We drove off. I watched the house become smaller behind us.

The air was full of salt.

It tasted like tears.

5

WE DROVE ALONG THE sea. I kept my eyes out over the water and turned to the sky, looking for more aerials.

But none came.

In the distance, up ahead, appeared a series of buildings surrounded by a fence.

The buildings were drab beige and low. As we drew closer, I could see military vehicles. And that the fence was strong, with barbed wire high, high at the top.

It looked like a prison.

"Is that where you're taking me?"

Mr. Parmeter had his own little girl. He wouldn't drop me off to be locked up, would he? Not after he was so nice and let me stay the night?

Maybe he was angry about what had happened to his sons? Maybe he didn't trust me after all?

Finally he said, "It is, but I don't want you to be worried. That's where everyone entering on this shore has been going. They'll sort out where you're meant to be."

Then why all the barbed wire?

There had been a wall at Faetre, too, but it had felt different. It was smooth, with nothing sharp on top. It had probably been for the privacy of the wealthy family who'd lived there originally. It had felt safe inside.

This fence was not about privacy. It was about something else. Maybe even being on display. People in brown and gray clothes walked within the fence, as if trying to get what sunshine they could out of the hazy day, as if, they, like me, were trying to figure out where they were. Whether there was anywhere they belonged.

"I'll stay with you as long as I can. Make sure you are properly seen to."

If he was right, and everyone entering the country nearby was being sent to this facility, then my friends would be here. They had to be. If they'd made it across the sea as planned, this was where they would be.

I held my bag tighter against my waist. What if all my papers blew out of the car, and when we got there, I couldn't prove who I was? They might not believe me when I said I was looking for a group. They might not help me find my friends.

At the fence, an Eilean soldier held out his hand for us to stop. Another soldier stepped up to the driver's side to speak to Angelica's father.

"I've picked up a child from Sofarende. Seems to be in an interesting situation. Got separated from a group with entry clearance."

"Entry clearance?" the soldier asked.

"Show him," Angelica's father said to me.

I rummaged in the bag and handed over my now-crumpled yellow entry card.

"This is you?" The soldier pointed to my name.

I nodded.

"Essential war work? How old are you?"

"Twelve." I handed over my ID card and my military clearance.

The soldier studied my documents for a long time. Was he going to laugh?

"Hold on a minute." He took my papers over to the other soldier, and they talked. Then he came back and handed the papers to me. "Step out of the car, miss. We're not sure what these papers are about, but we'll hold you for questioning and processing like everyone else."

My hand shook as I fumbled for the doorknob.

Angelica's father put his hand over my other one.

"I've promised my wife I'd come in with her. She's just a child, after all."

I stared at Mr. Parmeter, silently asking if it was true that his wife had worried about me. When his eyes met mine, I could see that it was.

"You have your own ID? We'll need that as well. Leave your vehicle here."

There was a series of fences to bring vehicles through, but we walked. I clutched my bag tight as we went through the first gate. At the second, we were met by another team of soldiers with guns strapped to them, who asked to look through my bag. I handed it over. Then they made us each stand to be patted down, to see if we had weapons hiding in our clothes. I didn't, obviously, and, with a slight pang of guilt, I was relieved that Angelica's father didn't, either.

"What are these?" one of the soldiers asked, holding up my thick stack of papers.

My heart sank. Would they take my papers from me, just when I was about to find the Examiner and return them to her? I would have failed at the only part of my mission that I understood.

I didn't even know what those papers said. Were they dangerous? Were the Eilean authorities supposed to have them, or were they only for our group to see?

The soldier who had walked in with us nudged him and showed him my yellow card, pointing to something on it.

"She'll go straight in to Reeve anyhow. She'll bring it all with her. He can decide."

My bag was handed back to me.

Angelica's father shook his head.

How could children be put to such a use?

A shiver of fear ran through my chest as we approached the second gate and the soldiers went to unlock it.

Megs? Are you here? You are, aren't you? In a few minutes, we'll be together, like we promised.

We walked through the gate. It was locked behind us as two of the soldiers escorted us toward one of the buildings.

I swallowed hard, had trouble making my feet take each new step.

A hand squeezed my shoulder. I looked up at Angelica's father, his expression gentle. Comforting. He even smiled a little.

I nodded.

He's brought me to the right place.

I didn't really leave you, Megs. We've been apart before, for longer. A couple of days is nothing. It will be all right.

We were taken inside the nearest building and made to

wait on chairs by the door. One soldier remained with us. Finally we were brought into an office.

A uniformed officer stood to greet us as the soldier took Angelica's father's ID and emptied my bag on the desk. He arranged everything neatly. He even unfolded my sisters' handprints and Rainer's blue world.

It was funny to think of the blue world, when Eilean might lock me up like we'd locked up Rainer in Sofarende.

A hand patted my back to calm me. Mr. Parmeter's.

The soldier left, shutting the door with a sharp clunk.

"I am Captain Reeve," said the officer. "You are Mr. Parmeter?"

"Yes."

"And you found this child?"

"Yes. She knocked on our door. Seems to have washed up on the shore."

"There are boatloads of Sofarender children washing up this morning. Their parents shoved them into the sea, hoping they would reach here."

"She arrived yesterday. She arrived before Sofarende fell."

"And with permission, I see." He looked at me. "You are Mathilde Joss?"

"Yes."

"I know of Rohbears, who signed your card. Head of Intelligence. You were working for this . . ." He peered at the typed name. "Markusen?"

The Examiner, as I always thought of her, because she had been in charge of our entrance exams to Faetre. "Yes."

"I know better than to ask the nature of your work. Or what these papers contain."

"Sir—I—I was hoping Miss Markusen would be here. And the rest of my group."

"The rest of them?"

"Yes, there were about forty of us."

He looked distressed. "Forty children?"

"Yes. Aren't—aren't they here?"

"No. No, they aren't. I will contact Rohbears myself, ask where they are and where he wants you to go."

They aren't here.

"Until then," he said, "you will be detained."

"Detained?"

"I have no choice in that."

"Now that you know about her, could she continue to stay with us until her group is found?" Angelica's father asked. "It would be no trouble."

"No, I'm afraid not."

"She's just a child, on her own."

"We have lots of children. And she doesn't seem to be 'just' a child, does she?"

Angelica's father shook his head.

Captain Reeve studied me. Then he said, "You aren't a prisoner here. Well, not exactly. But this is wartime. We have to be careful whom we let into our country. While you wait, you can make yourself useful."

Just what did he mean? When I'd signed on with the Examiner, I didn't know what she was going to ask me to do, either, but this was a stranger talking, in a different country. He hadn't picked me, like she had. I'd washed up on his beach and he didn't want me.

My thoughts must have shown on my face because he

said, "Don't worry, there's just a lot of normal, day-to-day tasks we need help with, handing out food, cleaning. Most people have a job. We'll get you a cot in the main room, with the families."

He looked back at Angelica's father. "Not that I need to ask, but this sounds agreeable to you?"

Angelica's father cleared his throat. "Of course."

"Thank you for bringing her here. You may leave us now. I'll get on to processing her case. One of the soldiers will see you out."

Angelica's father stood and held out his hand. "Mathilde."

I shook, feeling a small piece of paper between us.

I crumpled it into my fist and hugged him.

"Perhaps, one day, we'll see each other again. Best of luck until then."

"Thank you."

He left, and I sat back down.

"What's that he gave you?" Reeve asked.

"I don't know." I looked at the paper, since it wasn't a secret anymore.

510 Sealane

"I think it's his address."

"Add it to the pile," Reeve directed.

Not wanting to be in any more trouble, I dropped it onto the desk. But I repeated it silently, memorizing.

510 Sealane.

510 Sealane.

"It is true you'd never met or heard of Mr. Parmeter prior to your arrival in this country yesterday?"

"Yes."

He considered the address. Would he go there? Send other people? Would they search the house, scare Angelica and her mother?

It would be my fault.

Just because they'd been nice to me.

"How did you get separated from your group?"

I thought about how much to say, without having to lie.

"We walked through the woods at night to escape. I was . . . behind. I couldn't catch up."

All true.

He considered. Then he said, "I wouldn't want to have to keep track of forty children in the woods at night."

I let my breath out but straightened up quickly. No need to seem too relieved if all I'd done was tell the truth.

"I'll keep your money here, in the safe. And your documents. I feel like that's the best option, as you won't have anywhere to hide them. Do you know what they contain?"

I shook my head. "What about my paintings?"

He looked over the two papers, smiling fondly, for just a second, at the childish artwork, but then shook his head.

"I'll keep these, too. You know. Anything could be information, these days."

He was right, of course, and I tried not to react as he folded up my sisters' handprints and set them in the safe.

"Okay."

"If anything seems suspect, we'll isolate you."

I swallowed. "I understand."

He took out a new set of papers and my IDs, and he started filling in the paperwork.

"Sign here."

I went to the desk again and scribbled my name. I didn't even know what I was signing. Then he put my IDs with my other things in the safe and locked it.

He handed me several cloth tags. They said 4381.

"That's you. Sew these into your clothes."

I took the tags with numb fingers.

Maybe we *were* prisoners. I'd never been identified by a number before.

"It's just for records," he said, noticing the look on my face. "Records and keeping track of your possessions. We have laundry service. We want your things given back to you."

How I was supposed to sew them, without needle, thread, and scissors?

"We'll be ready for you to go to your cot soon. There's one more thing ... you may send out a message, if there's anyone you would like to tell that you made it to Eilean. It's a courtesy we offer."

He set a postcard and pen out on his desk, on my side of his desk.

Mother and Father.

I didn't know if they were getting the Examiner's messages about my well-being anymore.

I hadn't been allowed to communicate with them.

I had been separated from my group, but orders were orders. I didn't know if my message would get back to my family, but I didn't want Tyssia to get any information from me, even by accident. Nobody was supposed to know where we went. Maybe it would put my family in danger if they were getting suspicious mail from Eilean.

I thought so long Reeve leaned back in his chair and folded his hands, though he didn't look impatient. He looked like this was a worthy thing to contemplate. Maybe it was even part of a test. Who would I write to, and what kind of information would I include?

"Do you have an ink pad?" I asked finally.

"Of course." He slid it over to me.

I pressed my left hand to the ink pad and then to the postcard. I picked up the pen with my right hand and neatly printed my parents' address.

They would see my hand; they would see Eilean's stamp and postmark.

They would understand.

Assuming the postcard got there.

Assuming they were still there to receive it.

I handed the postcard to Reeve.

He looked it over.

"Welcome to Eilean," he said.

6

THEY RETURNED MY BAG with my coat and clothes and gave me a blanket.

A soldier led me to a room full of cots and people. Most of the space was open, but smaller, makeshift rooms were marked off with blankets hung over ropes.

The hum of languages made me dizzy. Sofarender! But so many conversations were going on, also in Tyssian and Erobin, and snatches of Skaven and southern languages, that it was hard to understand any of it.

How long would I have to stay?

Maybe Reeve would call that Rohbears person and he would say, "Yes, Mathilde! We've been wondering where she is. We'll collect her right away!"

But what if it went the other way? What if they were suspicious about what I'd done when I was on my own? What if they'd rather not have me after all?

The soldier led me to an unoccupied cot in the middle of the room.

"You are to report to the kitchen at two-thirty," he said. "Follow the main hallway to get there."

I nodded as he left.

At the next cot was a woman with a toddler. The little one sucked on a teething toy made of knotted cloth. "Hi, love," the mother said to me, in Sofarender.

Mother had called me love like that, sometimes.

I tried to smile but couldn't quite do it.

"You on your own?"

I nodded.

"That's okay," she said kindly. "Everyone's a bit lost here."

I tried again to smile. I looked around the room. Hundreds of people.

How had they all gotten here? And how long had this camp been here? It couldn't have been made overnight since Sofarende fell. People must have been escaping to Eilean for a while, but I'd never heard of it until I'd been handed my yellow card and told we were going, and that was just a couple of nights ago.

The buzz of languages was so overwhelming that my brain begged for me to curl up on the cot and fall asleep.

To pass the time, I fished in my bag for the tags. Then I looked around. Was there a station where you could borrow sewing supplies? How could they give us instructions to sew and nothing to do it with?

The mother at the next cot noticed me looking around. She reached into her own bag and found needle and thread, held them out to me.

"We don't get to have scissors," she said. She threaded a needle and broke the thread with her teeth. She held it out to me.

I struggled to get my tag sewn inside my hand-me-down sweater. Mother hadn't taught me to sew yet. Would she have started by now, if I were still at home? My stitches were big and uneven, the black thread coming all the way through to the front of the light sweater.

The woman's expression softened. She took the sweater from me and finished it, her stitches neat. She offered to sew the next tag inside the shirt I was wearing. I sat still while she expertly stitched it at the back of my neck. Her touch was gentle. Then she sewed the numbers into the inside of my coat and spare skirt, the nightgown, the extra underclothes, and finally, she handed me another number patch, rethreaded the needle, and told me to try to sew the tag inside the front of the skirt I was wearing.

"There you go, that's right," she said, watching. "The underclothes you have on—you can put the numbers in when you change, all right? Just ask for the needle and thread."

"Thank you," I managed to say.

She smiled.

"Is there a washroom?"

"Outside, past the play yard. Most of the children are out there now. Maybe you should join them? New Sofarenders here today. Maybe you will find someone you know."

A faint hope sparked in my chest. Captain Reeve hadn't *known* about my friends, but that didn't mean there weren't any of them here by mistake. If they'd lost their cards and ended up here and didn't know how to explain.

I stood up.

"Right, you go ahead, love. Down the hall, through the double doors."

Outside, children played in a fenced area under soldiers'

guard. But the children didn't really seem to be thinking about the soldiers. They ran around and around, the way we'd always run around the schoolyard back home in Lykkelig and during playtime at Faetre.

Beyond the play yard was a low, narrow building with a row of many doors—toilets.

Phew. When she'd said they were outside, I didn't know what to expect.

I looked carefully at the children.

I didn't know any of them.

I went to stand with a group, where a boy with hair the color of sand seemed to be upset.

"They won't hold him long. They didn't hold our father very long. He's back with us now," another boy was saying to him, in Sofarender.

"It's been three weeks!" the sandy-haired boy shot back.

The other boy shrugged. He turned to me. "You new?"

I nodded.

"What country?"

"Sofarender. Like you."

"They take your parents, too?" the sandy-haired boy asked.

"Take them?"

"They put some people in cells, if they think they're suspicious," the other boy said. "They take your parents?"

I shook my head. "I came without them." But something in my stomach squirmed, something more than just my hunger.

Reeve could have sent *me* there.

I'd spent enough time in a room like that before.

It had been bad enough during the day, but I hadn't even had to stay there overnight.

I hadn't been the prisoner.

Technically.

Someone threw a ball at us—a signal to stop standing and play—and one of the children in the group snatched the ball and ran off with it, the others trailing behind her.

The sandy-haired boy didn't run to play.

"They took your father?" I asked him.

"He didn't do anything!"

"I didn't say he did." I stared into his eyes.

His scowl faded. He scuffed his shoes in the dirt, then looked back up. "You came alone? Your parents just threw you in a boat?"

"Not exactly. I came with a fisherman and then he turned around."

"Mother came, too, and my brother. He's little."

"So why are they holding your father?"

"They're saying he's Tyssian." He glared again, fixing his green eyes on mine, challenging me. Was I disgusted? Angry?

I blinked back, to show my calm. "*Is* he Tyssian?"

The boy sighed. "He was born there. He grew up there. But he married Mother, who is a Sofarender. We lived in Sofarende. In my life, he's never been to Tyssia."

"Oh." I couldn't think what else to say.

He lowered his voice. "They must think it was suspicious, showing up when we did, a few weeks before Tyssia took Sofarende. They think he knew something about Sofarende falling that no one else did."

I swallowed hard. My group had had a warning about that, too. That was how I got to Eilean just in time.

"You agree? You think it's suspicious?" He sounded mad again.

I shook my head. "No. Not at all. Things were already bad in lots of Sofarende."

I didn't know why he was telling me so much. Maybe because I was the only one who hadn't run away.

"I'm Micah," he said.

"Mathilde." I looked around. "Do you know the way to the kitchen? I'm supposed to work there."

"Just go inside these doors and walk to the end of the hallway."

"Thanks."

I went back inside and found the kitchen.

There were other people working—mostly grown-ups, but a few older kids—scrubbing or peeling potatoes, washing dishes. I'd probably missed lunch while I was being "processed."

One woman was giving directions in Eilian and seemed to be in charge. I walked over to her and waited.

"Yes?" she asked.

"I'm Mathilde? They told me to come here?"

"Right. Okay. I'm Shella, I run the kitchen. You can fold those napkins into the baskets and put them out on the tables. Then you can ladle soup when the meal starts."

I folded what must have been a hundred napkins and set out the baskets.

When people started coming in, I stood by the soup pot. I filled each bowl with broth and soft bits of carrots and onion. The soup was thin, but it smelled good. My stomach grumbled.

When the line ended and finally it might have been my turn to eat, Shella said, "Now fill a dozen more bowls for the trays."

For those in cells?

When that was done, she told me I could eat.

"But wait—" She grabbed the bread from the rim of my bowl.

That wasn't fair! My stomach protested.

She spread butter all over the bread and set it back.

"Don't let anyone see that."

I nodded, too surprised even to smile.

After dinner, I went to wash and headed back to my cot. People were changing in the open if they didn't have a curtained area of their own.

No privacy.

But nobody really seemed to pause or even care.

Maybe that was one of the things you gave up when you had to run away to be a refugee.

I changed into my nightclothes in the open, too.

At nine p.m. exactly, the overhead lights were shut off. The children running around were herded by parents back to their makeshift rooms and cots and were soon settled. I lay on my cot, observing in the dark. There were other children without parents, of course; staff checked that they made it to their beds as they took the evening attendance. Someone glanced at me, made a mark on a paper, but she didn't say good night. She just marched away.

The family next to me had three cots. A brother and sister slept in their own beds and the toddler shared with the mother. She tried to rock and settle her crying baby.

"Excuse me?" I asked.

"What, love?" she said.

"Where do we go if there's a bombing?"

"Where do we go?"

"Where is our shelter?"

She made a noise that sounded like a hiccup.

Holding in a laugh.

"I'm sorry," she said. "I suppose you could duck under your cot."

"Oh. Thank you."

Did the people at the camp matter so little to anybody that they hadn't arranged a shelter for us? Or was Eilean just not ready for the war at all?

Aerials had flown over.

They could come back.

The noise dulled as sleepiness settled across the room. Grown-ups huddled in small groups in chairs, their voices drifting as they whispered.

It reminded me of something I hadn't heard in a very long time—my parents talking after my sisters and I had gone to bed.

I curled up on my side, clutching my bag of clothes to my chest like a lovey.

I had once belonged to a family.

I'd left them a long time ago.

Then I'd become a Faetre kid.

That was over, too.

I wasn't even really a good Sofarender anymore.

I didn't belong anywhere.

Not even in this room of people with nowhere to go.

I was still different from them, still separate.

They probably hadn't ended up here because they'd done something wrong.

The voices of the parents died away over the hours as they slowly made their way to their own cots.

I stared up at the dark ceiling, which was so black I might have been staring into the night sky.

A sky dark and starless.

A sky without a single light.

7

I GOBBLED MY MORNING porridge—it was always porridge—and hurried to Captain Reeve's office.

One of the soldiers outside his door sighed when he saw me. "Nothing today, Mathilde."

"You say that every day." For fourteen long days. I glared at him, arms crossed over my chest.

"Okay," he said. "I'll go ask."

He disappeared into the office and returned a minute later.

"Nothing. We'll find *you*, I promise. It's getting so crowded, we'd be happy to get even one of you out of here."

It *was* getting more crowded. All the cots in the big family room were in use. And there were more cots lining the hallways. I served twice as many soup bowls at dinner. My arm hurt from ladling.

I glared at him again. *You'd better tell me right away.*

He reached into his pocket and held out his hand.

A candy!

I snatched it and smiled. "Thank you!"

I raced out to the yard with the other kids. I slipped the candy into my mouth, which immediately watered at the fake sugar and pretend berry flavor.

Micah saw me and came over. I drew as much out of the candy as I could, spat it into my hand, and held it out to him.

He cracked it on his back molars and gave half back to me.

Then we sat against the wall of the building, slurping our candy in the shade.

Mother would have been horrified at our manner of sharing.

But I'm alive, Mother. I'm alive, isn't that all you could ask for?

I looked up into the sky, the same sky she was under. Though mine was bright blue, and I pictured the sky over Sofarende gray with smoke. Covering a land smoldering red from bombings.

"Any news?"

"No. You?"

"No."

We sat in silence, savoring our candies. Micah stuck out his tongue, showing the remaining pink sliver of the sweet. I stuck my tongue out, too. My sliver was bigger. It always was, when we checked. Either I managed to eat my candy more slowly, or Micah always gave me the bigger piece on purpose.

Eventually the slivers faded away.

"Ready?" Micah asked.

"Of course," I said.

We hopped up and joined the others in the combination

of racing and tag that seemed to go on all day, like a constantly flowing river of children.

The yard just wasn't big enough anymore, so we ran through the series of fenced areas, the hanging laundry, the showers and toilets, the long hallways of locked doors.

"Get out of here, kids!" a soldier yelled. Like always.

We weren't allowed to be there.

In the minute we had, kids screamed the names of their locked-up loved ones.

Micah and I always yelled the same: for his father.

"Wilhem!"

"Wilhem!"

With the shouting and the pounding feet, we never heard any replies.

We hurried on through all the large dormitories—the ones for single men and women, the family room, and, finally, back out into the yard. Some of the kids stopped there, panting, and others started the loop all over again.

I stopped to catch my breath, and Micah stopped, too.

"Why doesn't he answer?" he asked.

"He can't hear us," I said. "None of them can. That's what being in isolation means. No talking, in or out."

Micah looked me over carefully. While he had me beat on life at the camp, I could tell sometimes he was surprised by the things I knew.

I tried again. "It's so noisy in that hallway, with everyone running and shouting. Can *you* make out much of anything?"

"Then why do you help me yell, instead of just telling me it's pointless?"

I shrugged. Yelling was part of the game. It felt good. And if I was on anyone's side, it was Micah's. I didn't have my own parent here to yell for. That I knew of. Maybe I should yell for other kids from Faetre. For Megs.

I looked at the kids who weren't running. They stood in huddles, talking.

New kids again. I scanned every face, but I didn't know any of them. No sisters. No friends from Faetre.

For a week, kids from Sofarende had arrived every day, looking as if they weren't quite sure where they had ended up. They were quiet, too. Remembering their mothers or fathers putting them in a boat and shoving them into the sea, hoping it was the right thing to do, choosing to believe it was the best chance they had? The same choice my parents had made when they'd sent me away to the army.

Were there kids who hadn't made it? Who'd been hit by dybnauts? Who'd crashed in the water? Who'd had to swim but had no buoy like I did? Who'd been pulled by the currents back to Sofarende?

What would happen to the ones who'd gotten this far? At least I had people in Eilean to look for.

But what was really scary was that, in the last three days, fewer new kids had been showing up.

Like the northern coast of Sofarende was being sealed.

At lunchtime, I reported to the kitchen.

I didn't mind the work. When people left the cafeteria, they looked less hungry.

Micah was always complaining about his job. Cleaning the toilets. "They gave it to me because I'm part Tyssian."

A bag of potatoes waited for me. Shella gave me a smile and a pat on the shoulder as I passed.

Potatoes scraped skinless, I rinsed them and brought Shella the pot.

"We'll be using the skins soon enough. There's too many people to feed. Grab a bread basket."

I lifted the huge basket. We couldn't just leave bread out anymore, because people had been taking too much. Shella often let me pass it, because she knew I wouldn't show favoritism. Micah was my only friend.

The cafeteria was crowded and noisy. All ages, sitting in groups by the language they spoke—or maybe where they came from. I understood everyone as they asked me for an extra slice, for a grandma or a son who hadn't made it into the cafeteria yet or had to stay back at the cots, but playing dumb was a good game. I would give them a smile and move on as if I couldn't understand.

I wasn't allowed to listen to these stories. Food was brought to anyone who couldn't walk to the cafeteria. And if kids didn't stop playing to come eat, that was too bad for them.

I turned and nearly dropped my basket.

Annevi.

Wearing the neat navy uniform of Eilean's military.

She smiled.

"We've been looking everywhere for you."

8

"BREAD HERE? HEY! GIRL!" said a man at the table next to me.

"Sorry." I handed him bread.

Annevi sighed impatiently. She took my basket and set it on the table. "Help yourself," she said. "Come on, let's go see Captain Reeve and get you out of here."

"I went to his office already today and they said there was no news."

"I guess that changed."

"How did you get here? *Where's everyone else?*"

She punched my arm. "Everyone else? A better question is, where have *you* been?"

"*Me?* I've been right here."

"There were rumors you went on a super-secret mission."

My mouth dropped open.

It felt like the past few weeks had been months and months, and that my group had vanished. But that was backward. *I'd* been the one who'd gone missing.

"Megs? Did she make it over with you?"

"Who?"

I glared at her.

She laughed. "Yes, you worrywart. Come on."

Annevi grabbed my hand and dragged me along.

Then she stopped and I crashed into her.

"Actually," she said, "you lead. I don't know the way."

"Where are we going?" I asked.

"To Captain Reeve. To tell him I found you."

I sighed. "This way."

The soldiers let me through this time.

Captain Reeve was behind his desk.

"Ah, good, you found each other. Annevi, have you explained to Mathilde?"

"Not really," Annevi answered. "We came right to see you."

They *knew* each other?

"Mathilde, I finally spoke to your supervisor, Markusen, this morning. She was relieved to hear that we had you."

I stared at him.

"She sent Annevi to get you right away. You've been vouched for—you'll get your clearance and we'll discharge you from the camp immediately."

A wave of relief flowed through me—she *did* want to see me. Then a squeeze of panic—maybe she wanted to yell at me.

Reeve opened the safe and set all my papers, paintings, and money on the desk. He put a new piece of paper, a dismissal form with his signature, on top. He slid the pile across to me and I picked them up.

"Can I just say goodbye to someone?" I asked.

Micah's arms were interlocked with another boy's. They spun, shoving each other in a new direction every few seconds.

"Micah!" I called.

They broke apart. The other boy scampered off as I ran to Micah.

"What was that about?"

"What do you think?" Micah scrubbed his face with his graying shirtsleeve.

"Oh."

It didn't seem like the best time to tell him my news. But it was now, or not at all. Not at all seemed worse.

"Micah?"

"What?"

"I'm leaving."

"Where are you going?"

"I don't know. With my friends. They found me and I'm supposed to go with them."

"Fine then, go. Leave me here."

"That's not fair. I don't want you to have to stay here. But what am I supposed to do?"

He looked past me to Annevi, watching us from the doorway in her uniform.

"That your friend?"

"Yes."

Micah thumped my shoulder with his as he shoved past and ran off into the yard.

Annevi trailed after me as I headed to my cot in the family room. I stuffed my belongings into the little bag from Angelica's.

The mother from the family next to me asked, "You found someone you know?"

I nodded. "My friend from home."

The mother smiled. "That's wonderful, love. You're moving on?"

I nodded.

Annevi and I went to the processing room. It was full of lines leading to tables of soldiers and clerks. We were directed to a table without a line. No one else was leaving.

Annevi held out an identity card to our clerk. An Eilean military card, with her photograph. The clerk nodded. I presented my identification papers and the form from Captain Reeve. The clerk studied them. Then he took out more printed papers and started marking those. He stamped with noisy metallic punches all over the papers, creating bold circles of red ink, and divided them into two stacks, one of which he handed to me.

"Welcome to Eilean," he said; then he waved over a soldier. "Escort these girls out."

The soldier led us out through the series of fences that Angelica's father and I had entered through. My heart felt lighter as we exited each gate.

But I turned to look back. Why should I get to leave, when Micah probably hadn't done anything wrong, and I knew that I had?

There he was, leaning on one of the fences, watching, forehead and hands pressed to the grid.

I waved.

He didn't.

I looked for Mr. Parmeter's car. There was no reason

to think he would be there, but part of me felt sure he would be. Like these few weeks he had just stayed, waiting for me.

But there were only military vehicles and more soldiers.

And two bicycles.

"I came on that one," Annevi said. "They found another one here for you."

Annevi stood next to her bicycle, threw one leg over, and hopped onto the seat. Then she balanced, looking at me.

I bit my lip and stepped up to the other bicycle, taking the handlebars as Annevi had done.

Go ahead, leg.

Go ahead. Get on the bicycle!

But my feet stuck to the ground.

"Come *on!*" Annevi said.

Go, leg!

One of the soldiers chuckled. "I think your friend doesn't know how to ride a bicycle."

My cheeks burned. It couldn't be so hard, right? It couldn't be harder than swimming in the sea. And I'd done that. My leg finally threw itself over the seat and I tried to land on it. When I'd caught the wobbly bicycle from tipping over, I froze again, not sure of what came next.

"You can't exactly *pretend* you know how to ride a bicycle," another soldier said.

The soldiers were laughing. Annevi couldn't seem to help smiling, either.

But the soldier who had led us out said, "All right, riding lessons, right now."

"Just give the poor girls a lift," his friend said.

"If we did that, she still wouldn't know how." He took my bag from my shoulder and tossed it on the ground.

The soldiers watched as I attempted to ride back and forth with my guide running along next to me, taking his hands off the bicycle from time to time. They applauded or offered advice or shouted that I shouldn't listen to so-and-so's advice.

Finally my soldier took his hands off the bicycle for good, and I rode all the way to the end of the fence. I stopped with a jerk but kept myself from falling over.

I turned to see them all cheering and clapping.

I smiled.

Okay.

This was going to be okay.

I rode back to them.

"All right, you girls can go." Our soldier put a bag strap over each of my shoulders so I could carry my things on my back.

"She went a few hundred yards and you're going to let her ride two miles?" his friend asked.

"Sure." He met my eyes.

"We're fine," Annevi said.

"She can always push the bicycle if she can't ride the whole way," someone suggested.

"Thank you for teaching me." The words stuck a little. Like with sewing and Mother, if I had stayed home, Father would have taught me to ride a bicycle. Megs, who'd been there a little longer, said he'd fixed a bicycle and taught Kammi to ride. I'd missed out.

I wanted to ride away confidently, so I took off in the direction the soldier had said. Annevi quickly pedaled ahead, standing up to pump her legs. I wasn't ready for that yet, but the cheers of the soldiers helped carry me forward.

9

I FOLLOWED ANNEVI, COASTING along, lost in the seaside scenery. Sometimes the light changed to show Sofarende across the water to our right, to the south.

And then I would remember where we were headed, and butterflies would swoop in my stomach.

Today you will see Megs.

I would pump harder.

But maybe today you will be punished for what you did.

My legs would slow.

I went as long as I could before I called out, "Can we stop?"

Annevi pulled off the road, dropped her bike into the dunes, and flopped to the ground. Relieved, I did the same, panting as I caught my breath.

Lying on my back, staring straight up, I could see nothing but the blue, blue sky.

Megs is there. Megs. You just have to get back on that bicycle.

I will, I will. In a minute. I need to rest, just for a minute.

I rose on my elbow to look at Annevi.

"How did you get here?" I asked. "To Eilean?"

She stared at me, like I should know. "We came on a boat. A military boat with Sofarender soldiers, but it was an Eilean boat."

"And after that?"

"We landed at a port town. We were held there for a couple of days. A doctor made sure we weren't sick. Our papers were checked. A friend of Miss Markusen's was called. Our locations were assigned."

"I'm—I'm glad to see you again," I said.

"I was—*worried*—about you when you weren't with us in the morning. After we left Faetre." She said "worried" as if testing it, not sure if it was the right word for her feelings, not sure if it was the right thing to say.

I stared at her. Annevi didn't talk about her feelings much. I'd always had to guess them.

"How did you get lost?" she asked.

"How did they find out I was missing?"

She narrowed her eyes. "I asked you first."

I shrugged. "I was late getting through the gate. I thought it wouldn't matter, but then I couldn't find you. I couldn't catch up."

She frowned.

"What about *my* question? When did you realize I was gone?"

"I didn't know until the morning. In the night, it was confusing. We walked in pairs and threes. You could only see one group ahead of you. We had to be quiet."

"Didn't anybody look for me?"

"Miss Markusen didn't want anyone else getting lost.

She counted us a dozen times, like you would turn up if she just went down her list again."

I lay back down and closed my eyes. I *was* going to be in trouble.

"She was mad?"

"Mad? Maybe. I thought she seemed ... afraid."

For me? Or of what I might have done?

"So, how did *you* get here?" Annevi asked.

"I did what Miss Markusen said to do if we got lost. I rode the train to the sea and showed my entry card to a soldier, who asked a fisherman to take me across."

"Well, that's a miracle," Annevi said.

Not that it was clever of me. I sighed. I had never been as clever as the rest of the Faetre kids.

"So, you didn't try to run away? You didn't try to go home?"

"No, of course not."

Annevi got back up and righted her bike.

Rest over.

The aerial intelligence station was gated like the camp, but the space inside was much bigger. It fit aerfields and aerials and an aerial tower, open land, and a large building with several floors, the highest rising above everything else, glass on all sides. The station sat right on the coast's cliffs. Exposed, but first to know of aerials coming from the Continent. Huge guns lined the cliffs. It would be very hard to sneak up on this place.

Dozens of military personnel in navy blue uniforms like Annevi's walked between the buildings.

The soldiers at the front checked Annevi's ID card and

my stack of identity and entry papers, and that we weren't carrying weapons, and then escorted us through the gates. We walked our bicycles and left them on a rack with others, and then were shown to the main building's front office.

"Ah, Annevi," said the woman at the desk. Her eyes shifted to me and she smiled with relief. "You must be Mathilde." She sounded kind, like Miss Tameron, my teacher from back home, and Miss Ibsen from Faetre. People who spoke the right way, who cared.

What were Miss Tameron and Miss Ibsen doing? Were they safe?

"Miss Markusen is expecting you. Her office is three twenty-two. Head up the stairs to the third floor."

Nerves ate at my stomach. I looked at Annevi, to see if she would come with me, but she scooted behind the woman's desk, like she belonged there, and started looking at a stack of books.

I clutched my bag as I went up the stairs. Maybe if I handed over the documents and whatever information they contained, it would show that I had paid attention the night we left Faetre after all. That I hadn't been sneaking off to do treasonous things.

But she would know. She would know everything. She always did.

I knocked on door 322.

"Come in," she said.

I opened the door.

She rose from her desk as I entered, a look of relief spreading over her face. As if it mattered that I'd made it here after all.

I looked away and dug through my bag. I slammed the

stack of papers onto her desk. Glaring at her, I dropped into the free chair, crossing my arms over my chest.

"Thank you," she said.

"You're welcome."

She picked up the papers and put them in a filing cabinet behind her desk.

"Do you know what these are?" she asked.

"No," I said. "And I don't want to know. Now you have them. I did what I was supposed to."

"Yes, I see you did." She studied me and I stared back at her.

It would be better if I asked her. If I played dumb.

"What happened to Rainer?"

She looked at her folded hands, then back up at me. "I'm not actually sure what happened to Rainer. He's not at Faetre anymore. But then, nobody is."

She studied me again.

"How was it you came to be separated from us?"

She knew.

She knew she knew she knew.

I looked at my shoes. "I guess I didn't keep up."

"Megs did. I was very surprised to see her without you when we stopped to count everyone. You used to be inseparable. I thought maybe you had tried to go home, but why would you go home without her?"

I swallowed. She was right.

Home wouldn't be home without Megs.

Nowhere could be home without Megs.

The Examiner looked at me for a few minutes, waiting for me to say something else. Finally she said, "She's here. Perhaps you'd like to go see her now? And the others?"

Yes, I would like that very much. Of course I would.

But why were my hands shaking? Why, after coming all this way, after telling Megs I would catch up and crossing that sea passage, after waiting in a camp for weeks, did I just want to stay in this chair?

I sighed.

"They're in five thirteen. Same staircase, just keep going. I'll join you in a few minutes."

I nodded and got up.

I recognized her, even from the back, even if things had changed. Even though the last few weeks had felt like a lifetime.

Her hair had been trimmed, unlike mine, which had been left to grow in scraggles. She was wearing the navy uniform and huge, heavy headphones.

She sat at attention, watching images blink and change on a screen in front of her.

I couldn't help it; warmth flooded through me.

She was okay.

And I had made it. I had caught up. I'd kept my promise. Things would be all right now.

"Megs," I said.

She couldn't hear me through the headset.

"Megs?" I said again, but my voice wasn't coming out any louder.

It was stuck small, the way it got when I tried to call out in my nightmares.

The boy next to her noticed me and poked her arm.

She turned.

In the instant it took her to see me, a smile lit her face.

Just as quickly, it was gone.

She looked into me, so deep and so hard.

Reading me.

Then telling me.

I stared back. Sinking through the floor. The cliffs. All the way to the icy sea.

What can I tell you?

I'm sorry?

Please, please, don't hate me?

I didn't really choose him over you. I didn't turn and run when you needed me.

Lies.

I tried to keep holding her eyes with mine.

Megs?

"Mathilde!"

Arms surrounded me. Squeezed tight.

But Megs hadn't moved.

It wasn't her hugging me.

"Gunnar," I said, pulling back.

"Mathilde! We didn't know what happened to you!"

In the second I had looked away from Megs to take in my other friend, she had turned away from me, back to her work.

The Examiner came into the room. She saw me standing with Gunnar, saw Megs facing the other way.

"Megs," she said. "Did you see your friend is here?"

"Mmm." Megs kept her eyes on her screen.

The Examiner looked between the two of us, thinking carefully.

She went to Megs, put a hand on her shoulder.

"You should take a break, show Mathilde around." Megs remained stiff. "Don't you want to catch up?"

"No," Megs said.

The Examiner looked back at me. *What happened?*

I could never answer that question.

But I knew.

It was all my fault.

I looked at the floor.

"I'll show you around." Gunnar took my hand. I sensed the Examiner noticing that, too.

"Thank you, Gunnar," the Examiner said.

Gunnar also wore a navy uniform, looking well scrubbed, his hair damp and combed. Even though my chest ached and ached and my mind kept reaching for Megs, my hand was very aware of Gunnar's holding it tight. Like maybe he thought I might disappear again, and he didn't want that to happen.

It was good to see him.

The station was a maze of hallways. More formal than Faetre, with everyone in uniform and more adults around, mixed in with the kids.

"No art room here," I guessed.

"No. But it's good here. They need us."

"Why?"

Gunnar laughed at my tone but then grew serious. "I'll explain in a few minutes."

The rooms we passed looked like the kind we'd worked in before—full of maps and charts on tables, telephone stations at the walls.

"You were in a refugee camp?" Gunnar asked.

I nodded.

"Even though you weren't a refugee?"

"They didn't see the difference. They didn't know about the yellow cards."

"What was it like there?"

I thought. "Sad."

"And crowded?"

I nodded.

Finally Gunnar opened a door and there were Tommy and Hamlin, and Gunnar's team who'd done bombing predictions. And three Eilean men I didn't know.

They crowded around a map of Sofarende like the ones they'd had back at Faetre, marked all over with clusters of pins.

"We found Mathilde!" Gunnar announced.

"Hi," Tommy said, not breaking his focus.

Hamlin looked up for a second. "Hi."

The other boys only grunted. We'd never quite understood each other. It probably didn't matter to them that I'd been found. They wouldn't have even noticed I was missing.

I stood over the map, uneasy.

"Brid and Caelyn aren't here," Gunnar said. "I mean, they're in Eilean, but farther inland, at Intel HQ. Fredericka, too. Miss Markusen just got back from taking them."

I would miss Brid and Caelyn. But I couldn't look away from the map. Something was wrong.

"Here?" A boy pointed.

"No, that's pretty much wiped out," Hamlin said.

They started arguing. Like the old days. The familiar sound was almost comforting, but, as always, their debates cut into me with dark edges. The nightmare colors slashed through my vision as the blood drained from my head.

"Gunnar?" I asked. *Explain.*

"They need us," he whispered, "because nobody knows better than we do where the resources are, where the factories are, where the vital lines of transportation run. When Tyssia took Sofarende, they spread themselves too thin. That's why they haven't started bombing us here yet. If we cut off the supplies they'd needed to gain by taking us, it's over, we can push them back."

"Gunnar?" I whispered. He didn't hear me. I tapped his hand. "Gunnar?"

"Yeah?"

"What does this map show?"

"Same thing as always. Aerial raids."

"But—"

He put a hand on my back. As if he sensed I needed help staying upright.

"You're bombing Sofarende."

10

I PEDALED FURIOUSLY, MY heart pounding.

But I couldn't slow down.

My legs burned from pushing the bicycle so fast up the hills. I pedaled the downhills, too, almost losing control.

And then finally I did, toppling into the dunes and staying there. I dragged myself to a sitting position and scooched along toward the cliffside. Then I just sat, unable to catch my breath, feeling at once comforted and overwhelmed: Sofarende was over there, bombed and battered.

Why did the "right" side of the war suddenly feel like the wrong side?

I turned when a flurry of sound came up behind me. Annevi and Gunnar, jumping off bicycles.

"Oh," I said, and looked back out over the sea.

"What's the matter with you?" Annevi asked. "You'd think you didn't want to be with us. Why do you keep running away?"

She hung back, but Gunnar rushed over to me.

"Thank goodness we found you. Where were you even going to go?"

"Nowhere."

I wished there were such a place. Nowhere couldn't be fought over. It wasn't a piece of land to be claimed by different sides, back and forth. It didn't belong to anybody because it didn't exist.

Which was the biggest problem with it.

We were stuck with the countries that *did* exist.

Who fought with each other for no good reason at all.

I drew my knees up and buried my face in them.

"Mathilde?" Gunnar asked, putting a hand on my shoulder.

"Don't you have cities to bomb?"

He drew his hand back as if I were hot to his touch, but after a moment, he set his hand on my shoulder again. "I know, okay? I know you don't like it when we hurt people."

"Megs, too?" I asked.

"Megs, too." He sighed. I waited. "Megs, she's ... she's the best."

Megs, Megs.

We'd talked about this kind of thing, way back before we'd even tested for places at Faetre. What would the army ask us to do? What would we be willing to do?

I breathed in, long and slow and deep. "You really think it's going to help?"

"It already is. We can see it."

I stared at my knees.

"I kept my promise. I caught up, like I said. I kept my promise."

"What are you talking about?" Gunnar asked.

"I kept my promise but she doesn't even care. It's too late."

After a moment, Gunnar said, "Come on. Let's go."

77

"Go where?"

"Back."

I shrugged his hand off my shoulder.

"No."

"Where else are you going to go?"

I had my clearance now. I could go anywhere. I could go back to 510 Sealane. Mr. Parmeter had said I could come back.

But I was bound to the Examiner and whatever she asked me to do. That was another promise I'd made.

"You must be starving. It will be dinnertime when we get back. Come eat."

I shook my head.

Gunnar sighed. He got up and returned to Annevi. They got on their bicycles. And then they just stood there, staring at me.

I looked out over the sea again, but the light had changed, and I couldn't see our country anymore.

It was gone, gone, gone.

I had promised to work for the Examiner for the whole of the war.

I'd run away twice.

And I had promised to be with Megs.

Like she'd promised to be with me.

But I'd run away from that, too.

I stood up. Found my bicycle.

And followed Annevi and Gunnar back to the aerial station.

11

THE EXAMINER HAD TO meet us at the gate, because I'd left without any of my papers, so I couldn't get back in. She had them, though, with my bag, which I had left in her office.

"Thank you, Annevi and Gunnar. Walk her bicycle to the rack with yours, please."

They both glanced over their shoulders at me, but as they got farther away, they didn't turn again.

I looked back at the Examiner, who was studying me.

"Shall we?" she asked.

"Shall we what?"

"Walk." She held out her hand along a path leading away from the main building. "Talk."

I started down the path.

"You seem to have developed a habit of running away."

I shrugged.

"I need to know where you are," she said. "I need to keep you safe."

"But what about the people at home?" I asked. "What about keeping them safe?"

"Ah," she said. "I see . . . You disapprove of what you've seen here?"

I scuffed my shoes in the gravel, keeping my eyes low.

"I would have thought you and Megs would have been happy to see each other. You've been apart for weeks. You might not have seen each other ever again. What am I supposed to make of her not even wanting to speak to you so suddenly? What's changed?"

Scuff, scuff, scuff.

"Mathilde?"

"I don't know."

"I think you do." She shifted my bag higher on her shoulder. "What happened that night you left?"

"I already told you."

"But you didn't include how you and Megs came to be apart, and what might have come between you."

A squeezing pressure flooded my chest and I couldn't take deep enough breaths. I stopped walking and put my hands on my knees.

"You can tell me. You *should* tell me."

I shook my head.

"You might even feel better."

She already knew. She was just trying to torture me by making me admit it.

"No," I said.

She waited.

"No," I repeated. "And I won't help you bomb people."

"Have I ever asked you to?"

I tried to stand back up.

"We'll find something that's right for you. But you do

have to stay here. Don't try to leave again." She handed me my bag. "Ask at the front desk and they'll assign you your room number. It's dinner soon. I'm sure you're hungry?"

I looked down at my shoes.

I was. Very hungry.

I hated how she always knew everything.

She turned and headed back along the path toward the main building.

I looked at the high fencing all around the facility.

All around me.

12

AT FAETRE, WE'D HAD our own rooms, each with a window, on upper floors.

At the aerial station, I was led to a staircase that went a couple of stories underground into the cliffside. Before the last flight, there was a huge metal door that could be slid over the top of the stairs and secured.

If there was a bombing, we wouldn't have to go anywhere.

Or a different way of looking at it: we would be sleeping in a bomb shelter every night.

The long hallway was lit by a few blinking electric lights. It had several numbered doors. The attendant opened door U210. The narrow room was lined with bunk beds on both sides. No windows.

She handed me a stack of sheets and a green wool blanket.

"If the mattress is bare, no one sleeps there," she said. She smiled.

Had she come up with rhymes for the things she had to

explain over and over? So we could remember them? So she could?

I took the sheets without smiling back.

"The cafeteria is open for dinner from five to seven. That's room oh-thirty-one. Back up the stairs."

I nodded and she left me.

An upper bunk at the end was open. I set to work making the bed. Under some of the bottom bunks were drawers. I found an empty one for my things. They would probably give me a uniform soon. Make me look like everyone else. At Faetre, we'd worn our clothes from home. The clothes our mothers had given us.

I hugged the extra clothes from Angelica's mother to my chest, just for a moment. Then I set them in the drawer quickly and closed it.

Some of the bunks didn't have drawers underneath. They had cans, jars, and boxes. Of water. Pickled vegetables. Meat. Crackers.

In case we had to stay down below a long time.

The cafeteria was a lot like the one at the camp, except everyone was in uniform. As I left the food line I spotted the Faetre kids mostly sitting together in the sea of adults.

Megs sat at the middle of one of the tables. There weren't any free seats near her. But when I walked by, she kept her eyes down anyway.

I spotted a half-empty table and sat alone.

I picked up my spoon and started prodding the weird concoction in my shallow bowl.

It was full of little sea creatures still in their shells, sitting in what looked like a puddle of dirty water.

Another tray slid in front of mine.

Gunnar. Who must have moved from somewhere else, because his meal was half eaten; empty shells lined the tray.

He watched me studying his food and looking back at my own, unable to decide what to do, and he laughed.

"Eilean seafood," he said. "It's smart, actually. They haul it up the cliffs. You don't have to feed it or take care of it, like cows or chickens. You can drink the broth. Or dip your bread in it."

He started spooning up his own broth. He beamed to show how good it was; I laughed because the herbs were all stuck in his teeth.

I looked around the cafeteria, where even the Faetre kids who had grown up in the mountains or the south like me were cracking open the shells as if they had been doing it their whole lives.

I dipped my bread crust into the broth and took a little bite. Within seconds I was prying the little creatures out of their shells and devouring everything on my tray. Gunnar tipped the rest of his bowl into mine.

The empty shells were pretty. Some were pink and so thin they'd ripped, but most of them were hard and deep purple or beige. I wanted to clean them and send them home to Kammi and Tye. They could line them on the kitchen windowsill.

The salty seawater lingered on my tongue, that same sea taste that always flooded me with sadness.

I looked over to Megs's table, but she had already gotten up.

"Gunnar?"

"Yeah?"

"If I did something bad, would you forgive me?"

He looked worried, but then calmer, like he was trying to stay calm on purpose. "What did you do?"

"Just"—I twirled my spoon—"*if* I did."

He thought. "I guess that would depend on what you did."

He waited, like he expected my confession. I looked down at the empty shells.

"Actually," Gunnar said. I looked back up. "You always like to do the right thing. If you did something, it probably wouldn't have been a bad thing. Not really. Or at least, you would have had a good reason for doing it. And I would have to trust you for whatever that reason was."

I nodded. I tried to look into his eyes, to tell him that what I'd done was that kind of thing exactly. That out of everybody, I thought he'd have the best chance of understanding.

"Is that why you ran away before?"

"I didn't run away that time. I hadn't meant to get lost."

"But today . . ."

He knew why I'd run away. He'd told me so.

And I'd said that awful thing to him. *Don't you have cities to bomb?*

He must have been remembering it, too. The look in his eyes changed. As he thought more, he started to look angry. I'd never seen him look that way. Not at me.

Then he didn't mean it? He wouldn't really forgive me? I opened my mouth to speak, but he got there first.

"You want forgiveness for what you felt you had to do? Maybe you should do the same for us." He picked up his tray and left me alone at the table.

13

MEGS WAS ONE OF my roommates.

When the dozen or so other girls started pulling on their nightclothes, I did, too.

But not Megs. She sat on her top bunk, three away from mine, still dressed, reading some papers.

A lot of girls were chatting, and the room was pretty noisy, so I didn't think anyone would pay attention to us. I went over to her bunk and stood on the frame underneath so I could talk to her.

"Aren't you going to bed?"

"I have another shift," she said, turning a page. She wouldn't look at me at all.

"Didn't you work all day?"

"Not all day."

"When do you sleep?"

"After the aerials get back. All morning. Now leave me alone. It's my break."

I lowered my feet to the floor, but paused and pulled myself back up.

"Megs?"

"What?" She looked up, blue eyes blazing.

"I'm sorry," I said.

She raised her eyebrows and then looked back at her pages.

"I'm sorry," I whispered.

Still, nothing.

I grabbed the pages and whipped them out of her grip. They fluttered to the floor, scattering at the feet of the girls who were still changing.

Everyone went quiet and looked over at us.

Megs was furious.

But I had her attention.

"I'm sorry," I said again.

"Prove it," she said. She curled up on her bunk, facing the wall.

Prove it? I'd kept my promise. I'd caught up. I'd found her.

I didn't sleep. I stared into the darkness—underground, with no windows, it was the deepest kind of darkness—and heard girls come and go in the night. Megs climbed down from her bunk an hour later; I felt her leave, her absence.

Maybe I couldn't prove it. I'd had my chance, when we left Faetre that night. To hold her hand and leave Sofarende together, to cross the sea together, to take our first steps into a new country together. I could imagine it, over and over, but imagining it didn't reset our lives and make it possible. It was done. I'd made my choice, and I couldn't fix it.

I could go to her, though. I could get dressed, go upstairs to where she was working. I could sit by her, find a way to help. Show that whatever happened, we could face it together.

The sea creatures in my belly seemed to come back to life and squirm around.

But if I went, I'd have to listen to my friends talk about the cities they were going to bomb.

The cities where our families lived.

The night dripped past, dark ripple after dark ripple, widening the sea between me and my friend.

14

"GOOD MORNING, BIG!"

I opened my eyes to see Father above me.

My nose, too, told me that something was different today.
Special.

"Happy birthday!" Father said. "Let's go downstairs and see what Mother made for breakfast."

Carrot muffins. Still warm.

Mother served me one at the table. She set out plates for Kammi and Tye, who joined us. Each of them gave me a hand-drawn picture. Tye's showed me with a huge head and birthday crown. Sofarender girls always wore a crown on their birthdays, though I still needed to make mine. Kammi's picture was, without explanation, a navy night sky with yellow stars.

"Thank you," I said to my sisters.

There was a knock on the front door. Kammi opened it and there was Megs, holding up a bag from the bakery.

"Happy birthday. Come out?"

Mother and Father nodded at me. I got dressed and headed out with Megs, arm in arm, to the edge of town and then into the woods where we always played.

We gathered the flowers for my crown and she threaded them through my hair so they would stay put.

"You make one, too."

"It's not my birthday."

"It doesn't matter. It doesn't feel right if you don't have one, too." She scrunched up her nose at me, as if I were being silly. "I'm the birthday girl, and that's what I want."

We gathered more flowers and made her a crown.

"I'm glad you have one," I said. "It's pretty, and I can't see my own."

We sat down and she ripped open the bag from the bakery—which was full of my favorite: raspberry-glazed buns.

I hoped she hadn't spent all her money to get them. But it was a good present.

"Thank you," I said. "You're eating these, too."

"Of course," she said.

We lay back on a slope in the grass, heads high enough to eat, and enjoyed the buns. The day grew hotter and the glaze stickier.

When we headed back to town later, Megs said, "Take my crown off. It really is your day."

She bent her head for me; careful not to pull her hair, I eased out all the flowers, dropping them to the ground. As we walked away, I looked back at the pile of them, wilting along the path.

The dream faded.

No, not a dream.

A memory.

Of my last birthday at home.

Someone was shoving my shoulder. I opened my eyes, but it was still just as dark with them open.

"Hey, get up," a voice said.

"Annevi?"

"They sent me to get you. Again. I'm supposed to take you to have your ID card made and to get your uniform."

"Can you put on the light so I can get dressed?"

She went back to the doorway and flipped the light switch. There were still other girls sleeping, but they didn't react to the light. Megs was in her bed, sound asleep.

"Come on," Annevi said.

Upstairs in the front offices of the main building, I posed for a photo. I had to show some of my papers again, but the clerk asked me questions out loud.

"Birthday?"

I told him.

"Not today's date. Your birthdate."

I repeated myself and added the year.

"Oh," he said. "Happy birthday."

"It's your birthday?" Annevi asked. "Why didn't you say so?"

I shrugged. I pressed my thumbprint to the back of what would be my ID card.

"Come back tomorrow. The photo will be ready and we'll match your photo and the thumbprint again. Okay?"

I nodded.

Then Annevi took me to the room where they gave out the uniforms. Properly suited up, I looked like I belonged with everyone else.

"Does Eilean have kids in the army, too?" I asked.

Annevi shook her head. "They're school uniforms, really. We didn't bring clothes with us and it seemed easiest just to get them all the same."

She led us back to the upper floors, where people were settling into their day's work.

"What am I supposed to do now?"

"I don't know. You can ask Miss Markusen. But she'd find you if she wanted you to do something in particular."

Gunnar walked down the hallway toward us. I froze when I saw him. But Annevi continued into the room where Tommy was already working.

Gunnar walked right up to me and stopped.

"I get it," I said.

"I know," he said.

"Friends?"

"Course."

Then we stood there. To break the silence, I said, "It's my birthday."

"Thirteen?"

"Yeah."

"We can celebrate."

I couldn't remember celebrating a single birthday at Faetre. When Tommy had turned fifteen, he'd been sent to work with the grown-ups. "It feels wrong, to celebrate birthdays."

Especially knowing that Megs wouldn't want to celebrate with me.

"Being alive another year sounds like a good reason to celebrate to me."

I shrugged. "What should I do today? For work, I mean?"

He thought. "Come with me." He led me into the room with Annevi and Tommy and the others. He took me to an empty desk and spread out a very large sheet of paper with some squiggly black lines on it. "Do you know what this is?"

"Sofarende."

"Good. Now fill in everything you know."

"What, like cities?"

"Cities, towns . . . forests, rivers. Islands. We don't seem to know enough about the islands."

"Okay."

"And take your time. Be detailed."

"Um, Gunnar? When is breakfast?"

"Breakfast?" He looked at the wall clock. "I'll get you something. It's a little late for the cafeteria."

He left the room. I found some pencils and erasers and started with my home, Lykkelig, and the woods around it. The mountains. I tried my best to put them in exactly the right place on the map.

I didn't know anything about the islands. There were probably a hundred of them. Maybe it was closer to fifty. But I'd never been to any or had to memorize them in school.

After what felt like ages, Gunnar returned.

"Happy birthday! Come up to your party!"

"A party?"

"Well, sort of."

He called Annevi and a couple of others over, and we followed him upstairs, where there were already Faetre kids, including Megs, standing around in a small kitchen. They all looked impatient to get back to whatever they were supposed to be doing.

None of them said happy birthday.

Not even Megs.

"I made cheese toasts!" Gunnar pulled a tray out of the oven.

Everyone seemed interested in that, if not in me. The

moment the toasts were cool enough to handle, they were gobbling them up. Gunnar grabbed one for me and put it on a plate. As soon as people finished, they went back to work.

But Megs hung around, eating her second toast slowly. So did Annevi. It was a very silent party. I wished Caelyn and Brid were at the station; at least they would be comfortable talking, the way they always had been at meals.

"Oh, I almost forgot. I made you a crown," Gunnar said.

My eyes met Megs's for a second before she looked away.

"I don't need a crown," I said. Gunnar had made me a hat once before, with big plumes like feathers.

He held out a blue-green map rolled into a simple ring. When I didn't move to take it, he said, "The girls at home wear crowns."

"We aren't at home," Megs said.

Annevi looked from her to me, then back again.

I sighed. Poor Gunnar had only been trying to do something nice. It wasn't his fault nobody else thought I was worth doing nice things for.

"Thank you, Gunnar. Of course I'll wear it." I set the ring on top of my head. "It's great."

"I need to get back," Megs said. She lingered for another minute and then headed out the door.

"I haven't worked all morning." Gunnar scrubbed at the baking tray. "I should get back, too."

"Thank you for the party, it was really . . . nice of you."

"That crown—it's your birthday wish. I figured you wouldn't make one."

How could the crown be my wish?

But Gunnar would have good guesses at what I would

wish for, better guesses than anybody. Maybe even than Megs.

I nodded at him. A lump rose in my throat as he left.

Annevi had stayed behind.

"Megs, she was your ... special friend from home?" she asked.

"Yes," I said. She was. She had been.

I took off the crown, and twisted it round and round in my hands until it got damp from my sweaty palms.

The crown was a wish?

I untaped it, unscrolled it.

On the blank side of the map, it said,

BE HAPPY, MATHILDE.

15

I WENT BACK TO work on my map.

Every thirty minutes or so, Gunnar stopped by.

"Add more details," he kept saying.

I tried. I tried to include, as best I could, things I'd only seen once, like towns in northern Sofarende I'd passed through on my journey to Eilean.

Finally Gunnar said, "Good. Bring it through." I followed him into the next room, where the walls were covered with maps like mine.

"Did everyone do one?"

"Yes."

Most of the maps—like my own—showed a flurry of detail in one specific part of Sofarende, and then a path to Faetre and on to Eilean. I knew immediately which one was Megs's, because the cluster of words and drawings matched mine, around Lykkelig, where we'd grown up together. And I could tell which ones had been done by Gunnar's team, because they were labeled most evenly across the country and included symbols and keys for things like "fields" and "factories" and "heavily bombed." Someone's key labeled towns as "obliterated."

"Check the floor, too," Gunnar said.

I looked down. A huge version of the map was painted onto almost the entire floor. It was gridded in both foot and inch squares. The details from all of our small maps were combined across its surface.

Gunnar pinned up my map with a note that said the content needed to be added to the big map.

"Who transfers it?" I asked.

"A lot of us have worked on it. Annevi's particularly good. She spends a lot of time in here. But until your map, we'd mostly run out of things to add."

"I don't think there's going to be anything new on my map."

"Of course there is. You took a different route to the sea than we did. That will help."

"But didn't Eilean already have maps of Sofarende?"

"Sure. But none them showed changes up to the minute we left. Actually, some of these changes have come in *after*. But our contacts—their messages aren't coming in as much." Gunnar frowned. He paced the top of the map, along Sofarende's northern sea border and the islands between it and Eilean.

"Does that mean our contacts are dead?"

"It *could*," Gunnar said slowly. "But it could also be that it's just hard to get messages out. There aren't so many radio transmissions anymore, and hardly any written messages."

"Are you going to use my map to bomb people?" I asked.

"We're going to use it to help Sofarende," he said carefully.

Obliterated.

I wished I believed him.

I went back to my room, opened my drawer, and reached under the clothes to the papers beneath. I sat on the lower bunk and unfolded them.

Grains of sand fell into my lap, but others remained stuck to the pages, coating them with grit. The water damage had dried them crisp and crinkly—the paint had cracked.

I studied Rainer's blue world. The image of the community was scarred. I traced the cracks with my finger. I wouldn't be able to fix it.

The world as I wanted it to be looked further and further from possible.

And the handprint painting . . .

Had I just given over all the rest of the details they'd need to ruin whatever was left of Lykkelig? To hurt my sisters? Mother and Father?

I checked how my hands fit over each little print again. No matter how much I tried, I couldn't match my hands to what had once been my own prints.

The door opened.

Megs.

She paused like she was going to speak, like she had been looking for me.

She saw me with my hands pressed over the prints.

She knew what they were.

Her expression softened.

She came closer, suddenly my dear old Megs. My best friend from always.

But then she saw the other painting on my lap. Rainer's. She knew that one, too.

Her eyes went steely and she stopped walking.

Tear it up.

Tear it up, to prove it.

But I couldn't. I picked the paper up and held it close. I glared at her.

Why couldn't she understand this one thing? That Rainer had needed me that night more than she had? That I had known she was safe with the others, and he'd had no one?

That I'd been afraid he was going to die?

That even though I loved her so, so much, there was room for other people to be important? To need me, too?

I put the papers back in the drawer, showing her where I kept them, and closed it. I met her eyes, daring her to take the blue painting and tear it up.

"He's the enemy," Megs said. "He's a killer."

"And what are you?" I asked.

What was I?

16

THE NEXT MORNING, THE Examiner called me to her office.

She let me sit and stare at her for a full five minutes.

Made me wait and wait and ache to get up and leave.

I didn't give in.

Finally she asked, "How are you settling in?"

I continued to stare at her.

"Is there anything you'd like to tell me?"

"You risked our lives just to get some papers across the sea!"

She looked startled. She folded her hands. Unfolded them. Folded them again.

"That's how you feel? That we put you at risk to get those here? That all we wanted were the papers?"

My jaw tightened.

She continued. "I'm sure that you will have realized by now that you are much, much safer here than you would have been had we left you behind. Had we left you in the care of your families before that. You want to know what's in those papers?"

"No! I really don't care."

"You're *acting* as if you care very much. In your packet, duplicated in Caelyn's, was coded information about your families. Hopefully coded safely enough to not be harmful to anyone if found. Names and addresses, so that one day, when this whole mess is over, you will be able to try to track them down again. Wasn't that worthwhile information to bring with us?"

My cheeks burned like she'd slapped me.

"Now, what else are you upset about?"

I shrugged.

"How about Megs? Are you two talking yet?"

She knew we weren't.

She knew everything.

"I'd like you to have lunch with her today."

"Why?" I asked. "What does it matter?"

"You two are happier when you're friends. When you have each other."

"What does it matter?" I repeated. Why should we be happy? Why would she care if we were?

"Have lunch. Talk. Tell her about whatever happened on your way here."

"Why? So she can tell *you*? If she was going to, she would have already."

The Examiner raised her eyebrows.

Oops.

I looked at my shoes.

The Examiner stood up.

"That's your assignment. Have lunch with your friend."

• • •

Around noon each day, a table was heaped with wrapped sandwiches for us to take when we had a break. Another table had mugs and canisters of tea.

I sat in a chair, watching the Eilean girls who worked in the cafeteria set out the sandwiches.

I knew they weren't thinking about it, but if they did, they would know that their work nourished people, helped them live. Their tasks were clear and manageable.

I got up and went over to them. "Can I help?" I asked in Eilian.

The girls looked confused, but one of them said, "Okay."

I helped carry in the sandwiches and arranged them in neat stacks. The girls went back to the kitchen, but I stayed. As the day wore on and people came to take their food, I tidied the remaining sandwiches and mugs.

"What are you doing?" Megs asked.

I jumped.

"Oh. Um . . . waiting for you."

"No, I mean, to the sandwiches."

"Making them look nice?"

She picked up a random sandwich, as if to show it didn't matter which one or how they looked, and filled a mug with tea. I did the same and trailed after her toward the door.

She stopped and I slammed into her, spilling some of my tea.

"What are you doing?" she asked again.

I sighed.

"What?"

"I have to have lunch with you today."

"What does that mean?"

"It's an assignment. From the Examiner. I'm sure she'll be checking."

Megs rolled her eyes.

"Where do you like to eat?" I asked.

Up along the cliffs, between the gunning stations, were parks for the station workers and pilots to seek some sense of peace—a little green and some benches, and, of course, the blue of sky and sea, if the weather was good.

Carrying our lunches reminded me of our thousand walks holding our lunch pails. We'd always eaten together. For years and years.

Megs kept her feet a pace ahead of mine, like she was in a hurry.

Trying to show me I couldn't keep up? Or that her work was so important she couldn't miss too much of it for me?

She dropped onto a bench and opened her sandwich in her lap.

I was slower to sit down and open mine.

The sandwiches were mostly bread, with a thin, pasty spread.

"That was one of my jobs at the refugee camp, to serve the food. I didn't mind it. Actually, I liked it."

Maybe Megs would care about that. How I had to live in a camp.

"Serving food? We got you an entry card so you could serve food?"

The wind whistled over the cliffs. The sandwich spread went sour in my mouth. I wished I hadn't spilled so much of my tea.

Megs finished eating and scrunched up her wrapper.

I held my sandwich tighter, with both hands.

"At least I don't hurt people! You're bombing your own country."

Megs looked as if I had slapped her. Then she shook her head like I was the one with no sense.

"Tyssia *took* it. This is how we get it back. Think of it as bombing *them*." Megs got to her feet. "At least what I do is going to help! What are you doing to help?"

"But Sofarenders get hurt. Who do you think is in the factories? Don't you think the Tyssians are forcing Sofarenders to work in the factories still?"

"You don't understand. This is how we free Sofarende."

"But there won't be anything left!"

She rolled her eyes at me.

She was right.

I wouldn't understand.

Not ever.

She slammed her crumpled wrapper into my chest, hitting me hard, right in the center.

"Be friends with Tyssians! I don't care! Come talk to me when you've won the war."

She stomped down the path back to the station.

I sat still, chest numb, inside and out.

I put away my sandwich; I couldn't finish it.

I threw her crumpled wrapper in the trash can, where it belonged.

17

A FEW DAYS LATER, I sat with Annevi in the mapping room.

She'd already added my map to the big one on the floor.

She was having me read the names of the islands to her from the atlas, spelling them slowly as she printed each letter.

"So many of them have Eilean roots," she said. "But they are Sofarender islands."

"That's because the islands are older than the countries. Eileans and Sofarers used to go back and forth."

She looked up at me.

"What? Didn't you pay attention in history class?" I asked.

"Sometimes," she said. "Spell that last one again."

I did, and she wrote it, but then she threw down her pencil, frustrated.

"Do you need the big eraser?" I asked.

"I wish I did. There's nothing to erase."

"What do you mean?"

"I mean, we know almost *nothing* about these islands. If anything, people went fishing or camping years ago. We have no idea if there are a million Tyssian soldiers on them now. None of us have been there recently enough."

"Why don't we go ask the kids at the refugee camp?"

"What?"

"There were still people showing up the day I left, do you remember? I mean, fewer people than there had been before, so maybe it was getting harder to get out, maybe there *were* more Tyssian soldiers watching the islands . . ."

"Mathilde, stop babbling. Last week, there were still people arriving from Sofarende? Who might be able to tell us about these islands?"

I nodded.

Annevi threw up her hands.

"Why didn't you say that before?"

"I didn't know it was important."

"Important? It's the best lead we have! Let's go ask Miss Markusen for permission right now." She stood up.

"I can't."

"What do you mean, you can't?"

"She told me I can't leave. Because I keep running away."

"She'll change her mind for this. It's brilliant."

The Examiner gave permission. Though she made us wait about an hour while she telephoned back and forth with Captain Reeve, making the arrangements.

We would ride bicycles there in the mornings and return by nightfall. We could go on alternate days for two weeks. On the days in between, we were to update the map.

But we each had a condition.

Mine was that I had to remain with Annevi all the time, even within the camp.

I agreed.

"And Annevi," the Examiner continued, "some of these children might be upset. If that's the case, I want you to let Mathilde do the talking. You just record what they say."

Annevi looked a little confused, and maybe hurt.

"We're all good at different things. This is what Mathilde's good at."

Annevi nodded.

We spent the rest of the day with Gunnar and some of the boys, making a list of interview questions they thought would be helpful. Some of them seemed simple enough:

Where were you living in Sofarende?

How did you leave Sofarende?

But some of them seemed scary:

Did you see Tyssian soldiers?

Were you meeting another party that didn't make it?

Did everyone in your party make it?

Gunnar printed us several more Sofarende maps and scrolled them up tight. He tucked them, sticking out, into our military messenger bags, the best way to carry them by bicycle.

My heart lifted, the way it always did, when I passed through the gates into the open world.

Two bicycle rides, every other day!

A taste of freedom.

Annevi turned on her bicycle to look back at me. "Don't run away on me!" she shouted.

"I won't!" I promised.

I didn't have a reason to.

I wouldn't want to get Annevi in trouble, anyway.

At the camp, we were met by soldiers who took our bicycles, studied our IDs. They let us in.

Annevi stood next to me as I stared at the camp entrance.

"We'll be out by the end of the day," she said. "It's not like last time."

"No, it's not," I agreed.

I insisted that we look for Micah first.

I half hoped he wouldn't be there. It would mean he had moved on, had been let out. That would be the best thing, really.

I wanted to see him, but that was selfish.

Annevi followed me out to where the children were.

"Micah!"

I broke into a smile as I ran over.

He didn't smile back.

"What are you *wearing*?"

I stopped running.

I'd forgotten about my uniform.

"It doesn't change anything," I said.

He raised his eyebrows.

"Okay, I know. But we came to talk to you."

• • •

Because we needed the table space, we were allowed to set up in the cafeteria between meals.

Micah had been interviewed before, of course, but no one had paid that much attention to what he had to say. They had been much more interested in his parents. He seemed flattered by the questions we asked, the notes we took, and that we let him label his own map.

"You don't think I'm going to lie, do you? You know, because I'm part Tyssian?"

"Of course not," I said. "Don't even joke like that."

After he'd told us everything he could, Micah got a couple of other kids to come talk to us. He stayed at the table, making introductions, prompting with questions.

None of the kids were like the Faetre kids. They didn't remember the precise details a Faetre kid would. Micah got us kids who were excited to talk. At some points, Annevi and I would look at each other with raised eyebrows as someone went on about a daring escape with dybnauts torpedoing their rafts while aerials shot at them from the sky.

"The truth, please," Annevi would say.

A lot of the kids would sigh and say, "Okay, it was like this . . . ," but one girl said, "That's what happened."

Annevi looked at me, a signal that I was to lead after that.

"Whose aerials were they?"

"Everybody's. Tyssian ones and Eilean ones. Fighting in the sky over the sea."

"The people you were with—did they all make it?"

She shook her head. Took a deep breath. "Just . . . just me."

"I'm so sorry." I reached my hand across the table and

held hers. She looked away and took her hand back to rub her eyes.

I slid a map in front of her. "Could you show me where your family was from? Where you left from?"

The morning stretched on, until the cafeteria began to get more crowded for lunch.

I looked around and saw an older boy, on his own.

My heart stopped.

I closed my eyes, counted to twenty.

I opened my eyes.

Definitely him.

I blinked once more, just to be sure.

Still him.

But he was different. His skin was slightly tanned, his hair sun-bleached. He sat up straight. He looked tall and strong.

No bars, no fencing between us.

I had stopped working. Annevi would notice.

I cleared my throat, picked up some pencils and maps.

"There's more people now," I said to Annevi. "I'm going to go to other tables and see what I can learn."

"Okay," she said. She laughed. "Just stay in the room. So I can see you."

"Right." I tried to laugh, too. As if it were silly that she'd been assigned to watch me.

But it was good that it was Annevi.

Megs or Gunnar would know exactly who I'd seen.

I walked over to his table.

His blue eyes looked so bright as he took me in.

"Mathilde?"

I set down my maps and sat across from him. "How are you?" I asked in distinct and careful Sofarender.

"I'm well," he answered, equally carefully. Some of his care seemed to be to hide the Tyssian accent I knew he had.

"Do you want an apple?" His soup bowl was empty, his bread eaten up. "I could go to the kitchen and get you one. I need to get my own lunch anyway."

He looked at me. Took in my uniform. "You work here?"

"Sort of."

"Like you worked in Sofarende?"

I nodded. "I'm interviewing people. I'll need to interview you, too. I'll be right back. Don't go anywhere, okay?"

A question in tone, but he understood that it was a direction.

That I was still the one who got to give directions.

He nodded.

He owed me his life; he owed me at least a conversation. We both knew that.

I slid my food tray onto the table and sat. I handed him the extra apple I'd taken.

"How long have you been here?" I asked.

"A couple of weeks?"

I chewed the carrots from my soup as slowly as you can get away with chewing mushy carrots. I think the soup had gotten even thinner since I'd left.

"How was your journey over?" I asked finally.

"Slow."

Rainer. His hair growing out. Wearing Sofarender

clothes: a striped sweater. He was probably pretending to be a Sofarender. The way he was talking, it sounded like it.

For good reason.

Captain Reeve would probably say he belonged in one of the isolation cells; for my involvement, I probably did, too.

I let out a long breath.

"You . . . kept your promise to me?" I asked.

The promise not to hurt anyone.

"Of course I did." His eyes held mine, his expression honest and gentle.

I wanted to believe him.

"What do you want to do if you are admitted to Eilean?"

"Take a long nap. With no dreams."

I wanted to do that, too. And then wake up to find Megs my friend again, my family safe and nearby. That the war had never happened.

"So no plans, then?"

"What kind of plans could I have? You know I can't go home."

"I . . . I might not be able to go home, either."

"You? What have you done?"

I stared at him, long and hard.

"Oh," he said, drooping back into his chair, understanding.

He was the reason I couldn't go home.

Two people, both without a country.

And I hadn't given up only my country for him. I'd given up my best friend, too.

I was trying to make up for it. Maybe he could help.

"I'm interviewing people about things they saw as they left Sofarende. Will you tell me what you saw?"

"Of course. I will tell you anything you want to know."

"Thank you."

The story started the last time we'd seen each other. We'd been setting out from the same place: Faetre.

I held my pencil poised over the place in the middle of the map. How would it look if I started his journey there? Every kid on our team would recognize it immediately and ask questions.

I realized my hand was shaking.

Rainer took it in his.

I took a deep breath.

Sitting and talking to him was so familiar. But touching wasn't. It had been possible only once: when I'd let him out.

I flinched.

"You are afraid?"

"Not of you."

My eyes went back down to the map.

"I see," he said. "May I?"

He drew the map toward himself, turned it around. Made a big circle in the middle of the country.

"I don't actually know where I started. But I was in the mountains, fleeing from the Tyssians. There was aerial fighting in the sky that night." I closed my eyes. I remembered that, too. "I didn't know where I was. I needed to change, because my clothes would give me away."

I'd forgotten that. I'd let him out in a very noticeable prisoner's outfit.

"I left my clothes behind in the woods; I stole some from a line outside someone's house."

114

I nodded. "It's okay. I understand."

"In the morning, I used the sun to decide which direction was north. I still did not know where I was, but I knew if I went north, I would go away from Tyssia and Erobern, and that was the way I wanted to go." He shaded in parts of the map. "I'm not so good at the geography."

He meant Sofarender geography.

"Do you know more about this part of the country?" I asked, running my finger along the mountain border, where I knew Rainer had been picked up when he entered Sofarende.

"Not too much." He wrote some things along that border. "Not too recent."

"We're mostly looking for the last few weeks."

"Right." He went back to shading in the north. "I went on foot. I tried to avoid Tyssian soldiers as much as I could."

I wasn't sure what would have happened to Rainer if the Sofarenders had caught him, but it would have been much, much worse for the Tyssians to have found him.

The Tyssians thought it was dishonorable to be a prisoner.

"Were there a lot of them?"

"Yes. In certain cities more than others. Marching in big groups. They were loud, easy enough to avoid."

"That's good," I said softly. "I was really worried about that."

His eyes flashed up at me, then quickly back down again.

"Did you go through the islands?"

He nodded.

"I did. I hid on an island while I repaired a boat. I pretended to be a fisherman. I don't know much about fishing,

115

but I never needed to prove what I was. The islands to the east seemed to have more soldiers on them, but farther to the west, they hardly had anyone at all. Or at least, they hadn't yet."

"Put that on the map," I said. "That will be important, I bet."

"You are getting this information from many people?"

"Yes."

"What are you going to do with it?"

"I'm not sure, actually," I said. "I hope whatever it is, it's the right thing."

He held my eyes for a long time.

"Tell me if I can be of more help."

"I will. Thank you."

He got up. "I have work to do, too. I'm helping make the new building out back. When it's done, they can have more beds, and more people. They will be able to help more people."

I had never heard him speak like that. I had never seen him stand up so straight.

I knew exactly what he meant. It was how I felt when I handed out food.

He took my tray with his.

The trays looked light in his hands.

"No, that's okay, I'll take it," I said.

He turned to walk away, looking taller than I'd ever seen him in his cell at Faetre.

I would keep his secret.

And my own.

18

THE NEXT DAY AT the station, Annevi and I started compiling the new information on the floor map. Gunnar and Hamlin joined us. It started to get crowded over the islands, so others just stood back and watched.

A stack of new papers slammed to the ground in front of me. I looked up to see Megs, arms folded.

I picked up the papers.

"Aerial photos," she said. "Of some of the islands. You should be able to see any big structures on them, any large camps of soldiers. Just in today."

"Thanks," I said as she left.

I sat back on my heels.

"Does that mean we don't need any of this?" I asked, gesturing at all the notes and maps we'd made with the refugees' help.

"Of course we do. We can see if it matches. Everything helps," Gunnar said. "Hey, this one's really good."

He held up Rainer's map.

"Oh yeah," Annevi said, glancing at it. "Mathilde talked to that guy forever. What was his name?"

"I forget," I said.

Gunnar looked at me, puzzled. "You forget?"

I shrugged. "We talked to a lot of people."

Gunnar studied the map, and his brow furrowed. I saw him take in the mountain passes on the Tyssian border; then the inexplicable jump to the mountains near Faetre; the odd, unclear markings of someone who didn't know where he was, wandering in the woods; then the incredible detail of the Tyssian military presence along the northern coast.

"Annevi," Gunnar said, "what did this guy who Mathilde talked to forever look like?"

Annevi thought. "He was older than us. Light hair and eyes. Why don't you ask her? She's the one who talked to him."

Gunnar met my eyes.

No.

No. No. No.

"Let's, um . . . come on, Mathilde . . . I want to compare this to . . . something in a book. . . . It's in the other room," Gunnar said.

I followed numbly.

He walked down the hallway until he found an empty room. He pointed to the open door. I went inside; he came in, too, and shut the door.

"Mathilde! You brought him here?"

"No!"

"You helped him escape?"

"No—I mean, well, yes, I did." I buried my head in my hands.

"Did someone ask you to do that? I mean, you had orders to do that? Or did you just . . . *decide?*"

I sat down on the desk. "I thought they were going to kill him," I whispered. "I couldn't stand it if he got killed. I wanted him to have a chance. That was all, just a *chance* to make it."

Gunnar sighed. As if this was just the kind of thing he should have expected me to do. Should have realized when I asked about forgiveness.

"Megs knows," he said. "That's why she's not really speaking to you."

"I think she guessed."

"And Miss Markusen?"

"She did, too, I think. Though she's trying to get me to say it."

Gunnar thought. He thought and thought. He sat down in the swivelly chair behind the desk and spun it and spun it. He ran his hands through his hair. Then he sat up straighter.

"I'm not saying that Rainer was a bad person. He was put in a bad position, like a lot of us have been. But you have to tell Miss Markusen. You can't go back to the camp tomorrow if she doesn't know. You have twelve hours."

"Or what?"

"Or I'll tell her."

He took Rainer's map with him as he left. The door closed behind him with a click.

19

I TOLD HER EVERYTHING.

Everything.

"Rainer's at the refugee camp?" she asked.

"Yes."

I prepared for the next questions:

Why did you let him out?

Why didn't you tell us?

How do you expect us to trust you anymore?

"Did you and Rainer travel to Eilean together?"

I blinked.

"No."

"So you didn't enter Eilean with him?"

"No. I . . . I only gave him garden clippers to get out of the fencing in his cell. Then I tried to catch up with you."

She stared at me. Then she laughed.

"What's funny?" I asked.

"Actually, nothing. That's a very serious thing you did. I'm sure you know that."

"I do."

"But—gardening clippers?"

I shrugged. "They worked."

"You truly trust him?"

"Yes."

"With your life?"

"Yes."

"What about with your family's lives?"

"Yes. I'd already decided that."

"You certainly did."

She was shaking her head, laughing again.

"What?" I asked. "Why are you laughing if this is so serious?"

"You're right, I shouldn't be. It's just that I try to think a step ahead of you, but you still surprise me sometimes. Where did you even get gardening clippers?"

"In the garden shed."

She stifled another laugh. "Obviously."

"What are you going to do?"

"Do?" She wasn't laughing anymore. She wasn't even smiling.

"To me. What's the punishment for treason?"

She paused and folded her hands thoughtfully. "We can discuss that later. For starters, I'm going to stop giving you the keys to the cells of high-security prisoners."

"What about him?"

"I'm going to have him collected right away and brought here."

"No!"

"Why do you object?"

"Because he's not hurting anyone. He's doing good

things. He's building a new house for more refugees. And it would be my fault this time. My fault that he would be locked up, because I told you."

"Perhaps it's your fault that he still exists at all. Do you feel bad about that?"

I shook my head.

"What's going to happen to him if the others at the camp discover what he is? Have you thought of that?"

"No."

"We'll bring him here. I feel responsible. Do you feel any better for having told me?"

"Not really. I still don't understand."

"Which part?"

"Why it was so wrong to help someone live, but it's right to bomb our own country."

She nodded. "I see. You may go now, Mathilde."

I started to get up.

"But . . . what's my punishment?"

"I said we'd discuss it later. At the moment, I can't see what would be any worse than what you're already going through."

20

SOMEONE SHOOK ME IN the dark.

"Why aren't you up yet?" Annevi asked. "Are you sick?"

"No. Why are you waking me up?"

"Aren't we going to go to the camp?" she asked.

"Are we allowed to?"

"Of course we're allowed to. We just got permission, remember? It's only our second day."

"So no one told you I'm not allowed to go today?"

"What are you talking about? Get up already."

I sat up.

No one had said anything to Annevi.

Then they didn't all know.

They weren't all talking about it.

I fumbled for my clothes in the dark and got dressed.

On the bicycle ride, the wind whipping past me and the wide-open sky above me filled me with guilt. It settled in my stomach as we entered the camp.

I kept my eyes open for Rainer as we started our work,

but I didn't see him. Not even as more people began to come to the cafeteria for lunch.

Micah found me at one of the tables.

"You're here again!" he said. He sounded much happier to see me than he had the last time. "Can I help today? Need some new kids? I could find some you haven't talked to yet."

"Did anything happen here yesterday?" I asked. "Or are there any weird rumors?"

His eyes went wide. "Well, they came and took a guy. We don't know what for, but people are saying he's a Tyssian spy."

"He's not." I sighed. Well, not anymore.

"How do you know?" He studied my uniform again.

"Is your father?" I asked.

"No," he said.

"This guy probably wasn't, either."

Micah considered.

"Thanks for offering to help. Do you know anybody who's gotten here really recently? Like in the past week?"

That night, Gunnar found me sitting alone at the map.

"Why aren't you at dinner?" I asked.

"Why aren't *you* at dinner?"

I shrugged.

"You did the right thing," he said. "Telling, I mean."

"I don't know."

He sat down, too.

"Gunnar? What are we mapping the islands for? Are we going to bomb them?"

"I don't think there's anything there to bomb. I think

we're looking for good points of entry. To land Eilean troops and be able to defend them."

"Oh." The tightness in my chest eased. "That sounds okay." I looked at Gunnar carefully. He looked tired. "Why *aren't* you at dinner?"

He turned slightly pink.

He must have been worried when I hadn't turned up.

I hadn't wanted to eat.

But I didn't want Gunnar not to eat.

"Come on," I said. "Let's go get you some sea creatures."

21

THE CHAIRS WERE ARRANGED in a circle.

We didn't have big meetings like this very often; we certainly hadn't had any in the six weeks I'd been at the aerial station.

Everyone was chatting excitedly, trying to guess the news.

When the Examiner came in, we sat down quickly and stopped talking.

"As many of you know, we have been able to weaken Tyssia significantly as she spread herself out over Sofarende. We're planning an invasion to free our country."

Everyone was still.

We all waited, wondering if this was a time to cheer, or to cry.

"When do we leave?" Hamlin asked.

Everyone looked at him, then at the Examiner.

"We won't be going. Well, most of us won't be going."

I could feel my pulse in my neck. I swallowed hard. Would she really send anyone back to Sofarende?

"Most of you will be able to continue working from here,

as you have been. That will be the best way to help. But we need a way to get the details of the invasion to our agents within Sofarende so that the attacks can be coordinated perfectly. Our usual methods of communicating with them—well, if any of them were breached, it would mean the end of the attempt. We would have to start the planning over. We would lose weeks, if not months. Those of you who have been collecting information at the refugee camp may have noticed that far fewer adults made it across the water than young people. It's possible the Tyssians weren't as worried about the children being a threat."

My heart was fluttering—*don't, don't, don't, don't*—but the rest of me relaxed.

This was my chance to show I was willing to give anything to help.

To make up for all the things I'd done wrong.

I looked at Megs.

"I'll take them. The messages."

Every head turned toward me.

"You want one of us to carry it, that's what you mean?"

The Examiner studied me very hard. She sighed.

"We'd rather keep you all here, safe, but it would be so much easier for a child to wander back into Sofarende than an adult. Or a *pair* of children." She looked around again. "We don't believe we will be putting you in any more danger than any Sofarender civilian is facing right now."

"I'll go with Mathilde."

The first of many voices—or perhaps just the one I heard best—was Gunnar's. I met his eye. Then I looked back at Megs, who was staring at her shoes.

Come with me.

Be with me.

Like you promised.

Wasn't this what she wanted from me? A bold action, showing I was on Sofarende's side?

I wasn't doing it to leave her again.

But having caught up to her location hadn't mattered.

I needed to catch up in other ways.

Megs, please. Can't you see I'm trying?

"Thank you, Gunnar," the Examiner said. "I know many more of you are willing. If we let the group get too big, it will look suspicious. This pair is perfect."

I was looking at my own shoes as the Examiner started to list the things that needed to happen with our different planning teams: our mappers needed to find us the best point of entry; our coders needed to devise the best way to carry the information.

People were patting me on the shoulders as they stood up to form their teams and get to work.

I realized someone was shaking me by both shoulders.

"You're a mapper," Annevi said.

22

OVER THE NEXT COUPLE of weeks, we mappers built our plan based on the stories of the kids who'd shown up at the camp: Gunnar and I would pretend to have been fishing and would drift back into Sofarende between the islands we thought were the quietest.

The coders had been at work, too. One day the Examiner called me to her office.

"This," she said, "is what you'll be carrying into Sofarende."

She held up a book.

It looked ancient.

She handed it to me.

I opened it. Flipped through it, expecting to find a note tucked between the pages, a handwritten scrawl. But there was nothing but the brown, printed pages of Sofarender.

"There's nothing in it," I said.

She smiled. "There's plenty in it. We made it just for you. We thought about what would be the most unobtrusive way for you to carry information on you. Hidden in the stomach of a stuffed lovey? Stitched into a sweater? Then we decided on this—natural enough to not seem suspicious, and upon inspection, as you just discovered yourself, there doesn't seem to be anything else to it."

"But—why does it look so old?"

"We used old paper. And fresh ink, of course, which we then dusted."

"How do you know they can't break it?"

"Designed by Hamlin, tested by Tommy."

"*Tommy* couldn't break it?"

"Not in the time we gave him. Should give us the time we need to call things off if it falls into the wrong hands."

We looked at each other.

Would *I* have fallen into the wrong hands, too?

"If you and the book were to be separated," she clarified.

"And how will the people we want to read it be able to?"

"A key sent separately."

I nodded. I knew that was how this worked, most of the time.

"Sit down, please," she said.

I did as she said, but a wave of worry raced through my stomach. What else could she need to talk about?

"We have a third person who has volunteered to accompany you."

"Megs?" I asked.

The Examiner frowned slightly. "No. Actually, it's Rainer."

"Rainer?"

"Yes."

"How does he even know about this?"

"I have been having long conversations with him in the time he's been here. You said you trusted him with your life?"

"I did."

"That is still true?"

"Yes."

"I think you were right when you described Rainer as wanting to help people. We spent a lot of time talking about you in particular. I think he is genuinely grateful for what you did for him, and would do anything for you. He volunteered to help you, and we're prepared to offer him asylum in Eilean following the war in exchange for this service. He's just done the trip in reverse, and he's familiar with the Tyssian forces, so he'll be able to offer you protections that none of us can."

"So you trust him, too?"

She nodded.

"We will leave a few barriers in place. You and Gunnar know that the book contains information about the invasion. Rainer does not. All he will know is that you need to get across. Then you will go your separate ways."

"So what happens after we land?"

"You and Gunnar will set out to meet your uncle."

"My uncle?"

"Yes, Mr. Olivier. You and Gunnar are his niece and nephew."

I nodded again.

"Once in his house, you will leave the book on the table overnight. In the morning, Mr. Olivier will go out, taking the book with him."

"That's all?"

"That's all."

"If he goes out, will there be someone else with us?"

The Examiner smiled. "Of course. Your aunt."

I couldn't help but smile back. But I would let her be a surprise.

"After you complete your mission, and your aunt deems it safe to do so, you may go on leave."

"On leave?"

"Yes, you may take some time off."

Time off? Didn't they want my help?

"Soldiers get leave. They use it to . . . go home. Or visit places they want to see."

"So you won't be taking care of me anymore?"

"No, not like that. We will always take care of you. But if, when you find yourself in Sofarende, there's anyone you want to visit, you may, when you're on leave."

Her words sank through me.

We had never been allowed to write home or see our families. We weren't supposed to until the war was over.

Either she was dismissing me, or she thought that maybe, after I delivered the book, the war would end.

23

I RODE MY BIKE to the camp. Annevi came with me, but she waited outside.

I think she knew what I had come to do.

I found him out by the fencing around the construction area. He liked to spend time there.

"Micah," I said.

He looked up. "Hi. Need more help?"

I sat down on the crate next to his. "I came to say goodbye."

"You just got here."

"No, I mean real goodbye. I'm leaving."

He scuffed his shoes in the dirt. "You mean you got a placement in another town?"

"No."

"Well, where are you going?" He stared at me for a few minutes when I didn't answer. Then he said, "Does this have something to do with those maps? Are you going to Sofarende?"

I swallowed hard.

"Why would anyone go back to Sofarende?"

I shrugged. "I guess so that one day you can go back to Sofarende, too. I mean, if you want to."

He shook his head, then ran his hands through his hair and pulled tight, like he was trying to yank it right out.

"Who are you, Mathilde? You came back here with some kind of 'special job.' And now you're going to Sofarende? So that maybe *I* can go back to Sofarende? I mean, what? Are you a spy?"

I sighed. "I'm not a spy."

"What, then?"

"I don't know."

"You don't know? Isn't that something a person usually knows?"

"You would hope so." I tried to smile, but it wasn't really a joke. Micah didn't smile, either. "I wasn't supposed to tell you anything at all, but I did, because you're my friend."

I held out my hand. He saw the candy, took it, unwrapped it slowly. Popped it into his mouth and moved it toward his back molar to crack it.

"No," I said. "It's for you."

"You won't share things with me anymore, then?"

"I *am* sharing with you. It's a gift."

He slurped at the candy with a suspicious expression.

"Will I ever see you again?"

"I don't know." In this war, in this world, it never seemed to be certain whether you would see anyone you knew again. Then, sometimes, people popped up, back in your life. "I hope so."

24

ON THE DAY WE were to leave, Annevi brought my traveling outfit to my room. A simple skirt and button-up shirt. A sweater, old and worn. The hand-me-downs a child in a Sofarender fishing family would wear.

Not just clothes: a costume.

"That's an expensive sweater," Annevi said.

I flipped it inside out.

Unlike a regular sweater, it had a lining. I traced my finger along the neat stitches, feeling for something between the layers of fabric.

No one else would see them, but I would know they were there: the Sofarender orins that Father had given me when I left home.

Annevi stayed with me while I changed, like she wanted to say something and couldn't figure out how to begin. But she didn't need to say anything. I just liked that she was sitting there.

I tidied my drawer.

I would leave almost everything.

My paintings.

My coat.

My uniform.

The bag and extra clothes from Angelica's house.

The Examiner would hold my papers and IDs.

I didn't know if I would see any of these things again.

But none of them, not even my beloved paintings, were the hardest to leave behind.

I headed to room 513.

She was alone, trailing her pencil absentmindedly over a map of Sofarende.

I sat down in the empty chair next to her.

She didn't move.

I took the pencil out of her hand.

She kept her eyes low, took a deep, choppy breath and let it out slowly.

"Come with me," I said. "We could go home together."

She frowned, her mouth wobbling like she was about to cry.

Megs rarely cried.

She still wouldn't look at me.

"Don't you want to?"

The two of us, walking down our street, which was by some miracle still standing. Walking to her door first, then on to mine, where Mother, Father, Kammi, and Tye were all happy and whole. In the morning, I would pick up Megs for school, where she was best in the class but all we were asked to do was write papers and raise our hands.

"No," she said. "I'm never going back to Sofarende."

"Why not?"

"There's nobody there who cares for me."

It was true that Megs's family life hadn't been like mine. The night of our very first bombing, her mother didn't even check for her. I was the one who had waited to make sure she made it to the shelter.

"I do, and I'll be there."

She glared at me.

"I do!" I lowered my eyes, and my voice. "I do."

Her eyes, filling up, fixed on Sofarende's map again. How warped was the image through her tears?

"Is there another reason you never want to go back?"

I reached for her hand, but she pulled away and stood up. "They'll need me here, anyway."

"Megs, please. Someone else can do your work. I ... I need you to be with me."

"But it didn't matter when *I* needed you?"

I tried to stare back into her eyes. I could take the blame. The hurt. I had to. Or I could never make up for it.

"If you won't come with me, please at least be my friend when we say goodbye."

She shook her head.

"We might never see each other again."

She cleared her throat. "Don't *you* have something to say to *me*? You didn't the last time it looked like we might never see each other again."

What did she want me to say? I didn't let Rainer out? I didn't pick him over her? I didn't keep secrets?

Last time, I had wanted to say *I love you*.

"I never meant to get lost. I meant to catch up. It was supposed to be a few minutes. A few minutes, Megs."

"But it was a lot longer than that. And it ... it ..." She folded her arms over her chest and squeezed tight.

A swelling ache pressed against my own breastbone.

Megs.

"It's just ... easier this way. Bye, Mathilde."

25

"GOOD LUCK!"

"Good luck!"

"Bye, Mathilde!"

"Here's your pack! Don't lose your pack."

"I won't." I strapped it over both shoulders.

Annevi hugged me longer than I'd ever seen her hug anybody.

When Annevi stepped to the side, I searched the faces.

Megs hadn't come.

The Examiner noticed me looking around and came over. She held me a long time. Then she handed me an envelope.

"Read this before you get in the boat. Then destroy it."

Probably extra instructions. I tucked the envelope into my pack, next to the book.

Rainer and Gunnar shook hands.

None of the rest of the kids knew who Rainer was, not really. They probably thought he was just part of the staff escorting us to our launching point. Even though he was dressed in fisherman's clothes like Gunnar.

The three of us climbed into the back of a military truck.

The children and the Examiner lined up and waved at us solemnly as we headed through the gates.

And still, Megs didn't come.

They drove us for hours, heading west along the Eilean coastline.

Finally, the truck stopped and they let us out at a cliff-side with a path down to the beach. The barbed wire had been cut.

"Everything you need is down there, in the boat. Try to push off around sunset."

Rainer and Gunnar nodded and shook hands with our driver.

"Thank you," I said.

The daylight was fading. We weren't to light any lights. Which meant I needed to read—and then destroy—the letter from the Examiner before the sun set.

"I'll be right behind you," I said to the boys. They looked at me, puzzled, but I held up the envelope and Gunnar nodded. He and Rainer started down the path to the beach. They needed to find the boat before it was dark.

I sat down on a rock with my back to them and opened the flap.

Dear Mathilde,

> *I know that you have had to carry many burdens. I handed many of them to you. I know that I expect a lot of you; I do of all you children. Of my children.*

As you undertake this mission, you will draw on your courage and heart, the way you always do. You will make your own decisions, as you always have.

Anything that happened in the past, is in the past. You are doing your best to serve others.

You will always be welcome in Sofarende, or in Eilean, whichever and whenever you choose.

I'm proud of you. Go well, and be well.

Yours most sincerely,
Miss Markusen

I ripped up the letter, like she had said to, and held it in my hand over the cliffside, where the sea breeze lifted the pieces and scattered them. As the scraps of paper left my hand, I felt lighter and lighter, until, as the last one lifted off, I laughed.

Anything that happened in the past, is in the past.

The boys were about halfway down the cliffside. I hurried after them, but it wasn't about catching up. I scooted past Rainer, tagged Gunnar, and ran down the stone steps. First to the sand, I took off running, dropping my pack yards before I hit the waves and splashed in.

The water was cold and salty, like I remembered it, and I gasped.

The water separating our two countries, which I had crossed as a traitor but would cross again, starting brand-new.

Maybe soon I would be able to see my family. I could make sure they were safe.

And I would have helped bring an end to the war, just like Father had asked me to.

Gunnar picked up my pack and ran out to meet me.

"You okay?"

"Yes!" I yelled to the sky.

Rainer caught up with us, looking from one to the other. Then he broke into a smile.

"Happy to be going home?"

"Yes!"

"Let's find the boat," Rainer said.

"Here." Gunnar handed me my pack and went back with Rainer.

I looked out across the water.

When I got there, the only thing that would be missing would be Megs.

We found the boat at the base of the rocky cliffs, filled with jugs of water, packets of crackers and dried fish, and Sofarender fishing gear.

It had no engine. It was just a rowboat.

Rainer and Gunnar dragged it from the rocks to the waves.

When we got it to the water's edge, Gunnar and I climbed in; Rainer gave the boat a shove and jumped aboard. The boat rocked and water sloshed its sides. I curled into a ball, but Rainer scrambled to the oars, sat down, and turned them hard to push us farther off the sand.

Then we were afloat, heading across the sea passage.

The water darkened, changed with shifting shadows.

What if there were dybnauts? What if we couldn't see them, but they could see us?

"Are we going to get shot at?" I asked.

"Not by our side," Gunnar said. "The patrols know about us. The other side . . . well . . . hopefully, the patrols will keep them off. Tyssia never did gain control of the sea."

We had much better information about the waters than we did about the islands. The situation on the islands might have changed since the people we'd spoken to had left.

Maybe the islands were overrun with Sofarenders trying to get as far from the conflict as possible.

Or maybe they were full of Tyssians waiting for us.

Without an engine, it would take a lot longer to get there than it had taken me to go the other way. But the currents would push us toward Sofarende. We just had to make sure we didn't drift too far west, out into the ocean.

At least one of us was going to have to stay up all night.

When it seemed like Rainer needed a rest, Gunnar and I carefully switched places with him. He curled up in the bottom of the boat to sleep. I kept my pack on. If we capsized and I lost it, our whole journey would be for nothing. Gunnar and I each took an oar, giggling as we attempted to synchronize our rowing and felt the boat pull one way or the other in response to our mistakes. The waves were getting a little choppier, but we'd used weather reports to pick the best possible night to travel.

It had only been dark for a couple of hours, but already I couldn't wait for the sun to rise.

"How do we know we're going the right way?" I asked.

"I guess we just keep going the way we were going," Gunnar said. "We keep the boat pointed the same way."

I laughed. "What if we get so turned around that in the morning we land back in Eilean?"

Gunnar laughed, too. "Mission failed for lack of training in rowboating."

"Rowing boats?"

"Boat rowing." We gave another big heave on our oars. "We could use the stars. Right now we know where Eilean is. Fix your eyes on the stars above it."

I looked to the heavens. There were no electric lights on the coastline to block them, so the stars shone brilliantly. I locked my eyes on them like he'd said, and as we pulled the oars, I felt more like we were going in the right direction.

"But they're so far away. How does that work?"

"Things that are far away can still guide you."

I risked closing my eyes for just a moment.

I reached for Father, Mother, Kammi, and Tye to pull me home.

I let go of the threads to Megs that would tie me to Eilean.

26

"MATHILDE . . . MATHILDE . . ."

I rubbed my eyes as I woke.

The boat bobbed along.

But it wasn't like last time I'd woken in a boat.

This time, the boat rocked me like a baby.

Maybe because it was a different kind of boat.

Or maybe the water was different.

Or maybe *I* was different.

My clothes were still damp from splashing in the water the night before. The Sofarender orins inside my sweater were swollen and crinkly.

The air felt crisp.

"Gunnar?" I asked.

"Yeah?"

"Is summer ending?"

Both Rainer and Gunnar laughed.

"Yes, summer is ending this minute," Gunnar said.

I opened my eyes.

"Summer always ends," Rainer said.

I looked up at him.

Was he scared? Was he heading toward an ending, instead of a new start?

Were we all?

Rainer looked away from me, but not unkindly. Like he was telling me not to worry.

"It is time for you two to catch some fish."

"I've never done it before," I said.

"I have," Gunnar said.

He gave me two handles of a large net and kept two for himself.

"I will rest now," Rainer said. "We can't use the oars while you fish." He pulled them in, and Gunnar showed me how to lower the net and hook it. Then we did a second net on the other side. We waited, letting the boat drift. Rainer passed around water and food.

An hour later, we checked the nets, and there were a few fish! I helped Gunnar pull them up. They wriggled all around. I wasn't sure how we were going to keep them in the boat with us, but then Gunnar whacked them on their heads, and they were still.

My stomach turned. Gunnar caught my eye like he was saying sorry.

We left the dozen fish in one net in the bottom of the boat.

Our cover.

Rainer took the oars, again.

Gunnar and I switched with him, again.

Within a few more switches, we came to the first of Sofarende's islands.

We were supposed to approach carefully, as if we'd been coming around the islands and not from across.

They were beautiful, green and bright and almost blue. Some were steep like the coastline of Eilean, but some offered small beaches or even grass.

"I like that one," Rainer said.

He rowed toward it. Gunnar jumped out with our heavy rope and pulled. I jumped when we were closer and grabbed the side of the boat. We pulled it up onto the shore, and then the three of us collapsed, panting and laughing.

My feet were on Sofarende's soil. Even if Tyssia said it belonged to them. I dug my hands into the sand. I looked up at Gunnar, who was smiling, too.

"The boat," Rainer reminded us, and we got back to work.

We dragged the boat up the sand and Gunnar tied the rope to a rock, because we didn't know how far high tide came up.

"Let's make camp," Rainer said. "And cook these fish."

I had firewood duty. Most of the wood on the island was damp, like everything else, but we eventually managed to start a fire. We skewered the fish and cooked them, laying them out on rocks afterward. Except for the last three; those we kept on the sticks and ate just like that, tearing at them with our teeth.

I loved every bite.

"We have enough for dinner and breakfast," Rainer said.

"Let's stay, then," Gunnar suggested.

The conversation was rehearsed. Sort of. We were supposed to discuss any plans as if just thinking of them. We were always supposed to speak as if we might be over-heard.

After our lunch, we were all so tired we curled up for naps. The boys slept longer than I did, so when I woke up, I took out the book and started reading.

This was also planned. It had to look as if I had the book on me to read it, after all.

In the morning, we loaded up our things, pushed the boat off, and went to another island. We set up a similar simple camp and hauled in another net of fish.

The boys went swimming, and I started hanging up our fish on a line between two trees.

I realized someone was staring at me from a few feet away.

A Tyssian soldier.

No, two of them.

I took a deep breath. Hoped it wouldn't show that my hands were shaking.

"Hello," I said, in Sofarender. "Do you want some of our fish?"

"Are you alone?" one asked in Tyssian.

"No," I said in Sofarender, choosing simple, childish words. "My brothers are there, see?"

I pointed to Gunnar and Rainer out in the water. Tried to keep my hand steady.

Rainer was in the most danger of all.

"No one lives on this island," he said.

"We came for the fish. There's not much to eat at home," I explained. "But there's lots of fish in the water. . . . Do you want some?"

I held up two fish.

"We don't eat fish," one of them said.

"Fish are good," I said.

"You need to go home," the other soldier said.

"That is our boat." I waved toward it. "It only makes little trips. We will stop at the next island so it can rest, and then we will go home."

Gunnar and Rainer had seen me talking to the soldiers and were coming in from the water, pulling on clothes.

"Yes, go home," the soldiers said even before my "brothers" got to us. "Be on your way in an hour."

"Yes," I said. "They say we have to go!" I called to Gunnar and Rainer.

They both nodded and started collecting our things.

The soldiers didn't even stay to watch us leave.

"Did the soldiers scare you?" Gunnar asked, using our practiced speech again.

"No," I said, catching Rainer's eye. "I just explained that we were fishing."

Only two soldiers. Tyssia *was* spread thin. They could hardly patrol the shorelines.

21

"UNCLE IS GOING TO love these fish!" I exclaimed, holding up three on a line.

The woman next to me at the bus stop wrinkled her nose.

"I thought all Sofarenders liked fish," I said to her.

"We do, but you don't have to wave them about like that. Don't you have something to keep them in?"

Gunnar gave her an apologetic smile. "We forgot to bring it." Then he turned to Rainer. "The next bus is ours," he said, reading the schedule. "At least, according to this." He smiled, as if to say *But who knows anything?*

The public transport in Sofarende was a mess. There wasn't much fuel. Roads and tracks had been bombed or blockaded. Most of the buses and trains weren't running anymore. Gunnar and I had a two or three hours' ride south into Sofarende to meet our uncle. It would be possible to walk it, if we had to, but it would take us another few days of play-camping.

I looked around at what we could see of the port. It was crowded, but it hadn't been bombed. There wasn't much for sale in the market. I clung to my fish. There were stale crackers in my pack, too.

"I see the bus coming," I said. I looked at Rainer. He wasn't even to know where we were taking the bus. "Thank you for taking us fishing," I said.

He hugged me. It was a good thing that pretend siblings parting in wartime could hug for as long as they needed to.

"Thank *you*," he said when he let me go. He looked into my eyes. He couldn't say all the things the thank-you was really for, but I knew them.

"Be safe," I said.

"You too."

Rainer hugged Gunnar, too, as part of the show.

"Say hello to Uncle," Rainer said. His Sofarender sounded so good; flawless, maybe. "I hope to see you again soon."

The bus pulled up. I managed to look away from Rainer. Gunnar showed our tickets and I proudly held up the fish.

"Kid, you don't have a container for those?" the driver said.

"Sorry!" Gunnar said as we scooted to the back.

"I didn't realize everyone would be upset about the fish," I said. Maybe we were causing too much of a scene about our fishing trip.

"That's okay," Gunnar said. "Uncle will love them, like you said."

The woman from next to me on the sidewalk looked around, spotted us, and then sat down way up in the front.

I looked out the window at Rainer. He was waving to us. Waving and waving. Smiling like he was happy. Like there was nothing to be afraid of.

Like he meant it.

I waved back. I couldn't wave hard enough.

I wasn't going to cry. Crying might have seemed wrong for this kind of parting. I was supposed to be excited about my fish, about where I was going.

But the real me didn't know what was going to happen to Rainer. Or if I would see him again.

Good luck!

Goodbye!

I watched him until I couldn't see him anymore, and then I turned to face forward.

"We're here." Gunnar shoved my arm, shaking me awake.

We were the only people who got off the bus.

And there was only one person at the stop.

A man in a hat and sweater, reaching out his arms to us. "Children!"

"Uncle!" I ran to him. "Look at the fish we brought you!"

"Those are lovely fish! We will have them tonight."

He caught us both in hugs.

"Your brother has gone on his way?"

"But he says hello," Gunnar said.

"Good, good. Come, we will walk to the house."

We didn't pass any other houses on the windy farm road. There was only the one.

And outside was our "aunt."

Miss Ibsen. From Faetre.

I had hoped it would be!

"Auntie," I said, remembering just in time. I wrapped my arms around her and hugged her tight. She hugged me back.

A real hug.

"Mathilde, you gave us the biggest scare running off like that. When I heard no one knew where you were—"

"I'm sorry," I said.

She let me go and threw an arm around Gunnar.

"I'm so glad you've made it. It's pretty quiet here. Though don't forget, we have the root cellar to shelter in if any aerials fly over. The door is right around back."

I held up my fish.

Auntie beamed. "Let's get those cleaned up for dinner."

"Clean them?" I asked. "We've just been grilling them and eating them."

"Not in my house," she said. "You aren't camping anymore. Speaking of, the two of you could use baths."

It seemed like the kind of house that maybe wouldn't have indoor plumbing, being the only one in the middle of nowhere, but it did. Gunnar and I each took a turn in the washroom, and I felt properly clean for the first time in days.

I came downstairs in a change of clothes from Miss Ibsen and sat at the table. I took out the book to read, setting it open in front of me.

"Hair," she said.

"I combed it," I said.

"It's looking long," she said.

Uh-oh. Miss Ibsen was a haircutter.

She came over to me, gently parted my hair down the middle, and quickly tied a tidy braid on each side.

"There."

It was how I'd always worn my hair, before Faetre. How girls wore their hair in Lykkelig.

I ran my fingers down my right braid. It felt both strange and familiar.

No one had braided my hair since Mother.

I couldn't even say thank you. The words got stuck.

Miss Ibsen smiled at me.

"Gunnar, why don't you set the table?"

She let him figure out where the plates and forks and knives were.

"What smells so good?" I asked when I could speak again.

"Fish cooked properly," Miss Ibsen said.

Mr. Olivier joined us in the kitchen. He joked with Gunnar. They seemed to remember each other. I'd never met him, but Mr. Olivier had been the grown-up who first thought of inviting kids to Faetre, where they could be safe during the war.

Miss Ibsen took a heavy, round pan out of the oven and set it right on the wooden table. The pan was full of fish with crumbs and tomato. My mouth watered and Gunnar's eyes widened.

"We grow the tomatoes right here," she said. "Maybe you can help me in the garden?"

Gunnar and I both nodded. She served us heaping helpings of the fish and we gobbled it up.

"Of course, we have you two to thank for the fish," Mr. Olivier pointed out. "It's a good catch. How are things out there on the islands?"

"Quiet," I said. "I talked to some soldiers."

"Did you really?"

"Yes. But there weren't a lot of them."

Mr. Olivier nodded. The information was useful. But we still all had to act like it wasn't information at all. We were to act always like Tyssians might be listening, even here, and continue our practiced, careful speech, just in case.

As soon as I was full, I yawned.

"I'll take you upstairs and show you the sleeping arrangements," Miss Ibsen said.

I got up, leaving the book behind.

My mission was officially done.

"Will you let Mother know we arrived?" I asked Miss Ibsen when we got upstairs.

"The mail and telephones have been a little off lately," she said. "I'm sure you know that. But we'll try. She'll know sooner or later."

I nodded. I wished we could tell my real mother, too.

But soon, maybe I could see her soon. And Father. And Kammi and Tye!

Miss Ibsen led me to a bed that was more like a couch, but the patchwork quilt was bright in the light from the hallway, and the pillow soft, so I snuggled right in. Miss Ibsen ran her hand across my forehead and said, "Good night, Mathilde."

I drifted, floating in what felt like the safest place in the world.

28

IN THE MORNING, I flew down the stairs.

The book was gone from the table, and Mr. Olivier was gone from the house.

"Good morning," Miss Ibsen said from the stove. "What would you like to do today?"

"I want to go to Lykkelig," I said.

She lost her composure for a second. Then she said, "Whatever's in Lykkelig?"

I stared at her.

Cold rushed through me, all the way to my stomach.

I had been told I could go wherever I wanted.

No.

Not exactly.

I could go where I wanted when my aunt said it was safe to do so.

I dropped into a chair with an angry grunt.

"Darling, that's right, I know you have other family in Lykkelig, but it's very far, and the trains aren't reliable right now. You'll be with me for a few weeks at least. Let's try and make the best of it?"

She put a hand on my shoulder.

A few weeks? Or would it be months?

"I washed your clothes. That's a fine sweater you have."

It wasn't fine. It was just full of money.

"Thank you," I said. "It was a gift."

"Well, it's very nice. You can wear it when you go to Lykkelig."

It would be enough to pay the fare. That was what she meant.

She sat down next to me. She poured a second cup of tea, added milk, and pushed it in front of me. She put a hand on mine.

"Waiting can be very hard sometimes."

"Sometimes . . ." I took a sip of tea in the hope that it would open my throat back up enough to talk. I sounded awful, trying not to cry. "Sometimes, the closer something seems, the harder it is to keep waiting."

"That's true," she agreed. "Help me with the garden, it will pass the time. You can put together a nice basket to take with you when you go. How does that sound?"

They were long weeks of waiting. The tomatoes were fewer; apples arrived and dropped all over the ground. Miss Ibsen insisted we wear our sweaters. Gunnar spent time outside with me. We cheered and waved whenever Eilean aerials zoomed overhead. Tyssia's never once came to meet them.

Then Miss Ibsen started to get news from her contacts.

Eileans had dropped from the sky with parachutes and took three cities.

Eileans had landed on seven beaches and opened supply lines.

It wasn't all at once, like the day Sofarende fell. It was slower, in scattered pieces.

But it was happening.

There were only two apple trees. I liked to sit in one, Gunnar in the other.

"Taste test." He tossed me an apple. "Get one of yours, too. Close your eyes and see if you can tell the difference."

I held an apple in each hand and closed my eyes. Immediately, I wobbled. Would I fall right out of the tree? I opened my eyes again.

"I know which apple is which."

"We'll do a blind test after. I'll hold the apples. This is just preliminary."

I closed my eyes and bit the apple from my tree. It was sweet and crisp and perfect.

"Mathilde," Gunnar said. "Open your eyes."

"No thanks. You told me to close them. Now I'm savoring."

"No, I mean it. Open your eyes."

I opened them and turned to see where he was looking.

Something funny on the horizon. Like moving trees.

Or . . . men.

Soldiers?

Miss Ibsen called to us. "Inside! Hurry!"

We ran. She bolted both doors. But we pressed our faces to the windows.

Tyssian soldiers marched by. Hundreds of them. They

didn't try to get into our house or hurt us. They could see us in the window. Some of them took apples from the ground. They marched by forever.

When the last one had finally passed, Gunnar yelled, "That's right! Go home!"

"If they're going home," I asked, "does that mean I can, too?"

29

I COULD HARDLY SIT still for Miss Ibsen to do my braids.

"Mathilde, you need to be prepared. Lykkelig may not look like you remember it."

"I know, I know."

"Even the people may not be as you remember them."

"I *know*."

She stepped in front of me, put her hands on my shoulders, looked me square in the eyes.

No looking away, no lying.

"I want to make sure you understand. Things may be . . . *different* when you get to Lykkelig. Different forever. In a way that can't be fixed."

"I understand." I stopped bouncing and stared back at her. "I do understand. But at least, then I'll know."

Miss Ibsen looked over at Gunnar.

"You'll keep an eye on her?"

"Of course I will," he said, checking the weight of my pack, which he was stuffing with food.

"Why can't you come?" I asked Miss Ibsen.

"I need to stay here, in case of other visitors. Someone always needs to be here. It's not all over yet. Please remember that."

But it would be soon enough, if she was letting me go.

"You may also go to Gunnar's family in Holtzberg. If you have nowhere to stay, please, please, please, take the train back here. I will be here."

I hugged her. "Bye, Auntie."

"Goodbye, darling. Please be safe."

On the train ride south, Sofarende became the country I knew. More mountains. Cities so smashed they no longer existed. Gunnar and I watched in silence.

"We did that," I whispered to him.

"Not all of it. But we will fix it," he said.

"Like Auntie said. You can't fix some things."

"Then we will build them new."

I didn't know about that.

The train lines turned out not to run the whole way, and we had to switch to a bus. And then another bus. And then we got on another train. It got dark out and light again. My water bottle was empty. I was so tired, and tired of switching. Was I really awake? Was this really happening?

But then, as evening fell, Gunnar said, "The next stop, we'll be there," and I was wide awake.

After all this, after months and months and going to Eilean and coming back, Mother . . . Father . . .

I will be there in a few minutes. I'll be with you in a few minutes.

When the train hissed to a stop I bolted onto the platform. Was this the same station I'd left from? I ran down the stairs and outside and looked both ways, trying to figure out what part of town I was in. But I couldn't tell. Gunnar caught up with me, holding our packs, looking around, too.

"I wish Megs were here," I said. "It feels wrong to be here without her. She'd figure out where to go."

"We need a landmark you'll recognize."

We wandered as it got darker out. So much had been bombed I couldn't recognize what was still standing. A city of gray shadows. Jagged lines. Streets blocked by rubble. Then unexpected open spaces. It seemed to shift and change on me, the way my nightmare always had. Each lone person we spotted might have been someone I knew, and I hurried toward them, only to find when I got close that it was a stranger.

"Wait." I put my hand on Gunnar's arm. "This . . . this was my street. I mean, is. It *is* my street."

"How can you tell?" he asked.

"I just can. It feels like it. I'm almost home. Come on, it's a long street, let's keep going."

Gunnar seemed uneasy, but we continued.

I tried to push out what was bothering him.

That this city wasn't safe.

That there were hardly any people here.

A gap where there should have been a house . . . another gap . . . another . . .

But the next one was still standing.

Mine.

"That one!" I shrieked. "And there's a light on inside!

162

They're here! Come on!" I grabbed his arm and dragged him. When he tripped, I let go and ran ahead.

I pushed open the front door. It wasn't locked. The light was coming from the kitchen; they were probably having dinner.

"Father! Mother! Kammi! Tye!"

But I stopped short in the doorway.

It was my kitchen, I was sure of it. Mother's pots on the stove. Her curtains on the window.

But the family around the table wasn't mine.

30

MRS. HELLER STOOD, LOOKING like she was unsure whether I was really there. She planted her feet squarely, ready to defend her territory.

"You're supposed to be next door," I said.

"And you're supposed to be in the army. Why did you come back here?"

"I—I got leave."

Gunnar caught up. He looked around, moved closer to me. He knew something was wrong.

"Where's my family?"

"They left."

"Where did they go?"

"North, I guess. Like everyone who left."

"What about Megs's family? Did they leave?"

"I don't know."

"Why are you here?"

"If you look outside, you'll see my house is gone. And this one was empty. . . ."

I looked at the children around the table. They were so

thin I hardly recognized them. But one of them was Kammi's friend Eliza.

"Eliza, do you know where Kammi went?" I asked. "Did she tell you?"

She shook her head.

I ran upstairs to my bedroom. Our beds were still there, our handprints all over the walls.

The tightness in my chest eased slightly.

I pressed my hand to one of the prints. And then another.

The tightness started squeezing again.

"Mathilde?" Gunnar asked.

I went to the next set of prints. I wanted to touch all of them.

"How?" I asked, my voice high and squeaky. "How am I ever going to find them?"

"Is there anyone else they would have told they were leaving? Anywhere else they would have left a message for you?"

"I don't know. I don't know."

"Let's think about it on the way back to the train."

"The way back?"

"Yes." He took my hands off the wall and turned me to look at him. "Mathilde. Mathilde."

I reached my hand away to one of Tye's prints again.

But Gunnar shook me, and I finally looked at him.

Really looked.

He looked scared for the first time I'd ever seen.

"We can't stay here," he said. "Like Miss Ibsen said. We'll ask whoever we can as we go, but we have to go."

"We have to go?" I repeated.

"Yes, come on."

I pressed my hand to the wall one more time. Then he took my free one, linking our elbows and threading our fingers, and led me downstairs to the kitchen, where the Hellers were still eating.

"How long ago did Mathilde's family leave?"

"Last week," Mrs. Heller said.

If Miss Ibsen had just let me go when I'd wanted to, I might have made it in time. We'd all be together.

"Did they leave a message for Mathilde?" Gunnar asked.

"Not with me. And not that I know of."

"Okay. Sorry to interrupt your dinner," he said.

Mrs. Heller paused, looked into the pot on the table.

"Do you want some? Dinner?"

I shook my head.

"No, thank you," Gunnar said. "Do you know where we can fill our water bottles, though?"

"There's no running water. You have to go to the stream."

Gunnar nodded. Then he led me out of what used to be my house.

"Where are we going?" I asked.

"To the train station."

I opened my mouth to argue, but he interrupted.

"Look, unless you can think of someone else to ask where they went, the best lead we have is to ask at the station if anyone remembers them. If not, we could at least find out what train routes are running from here to narrow down where they could have gone. Do you know how to get back there?"

"About as well as before. And we had more than one, you know."

"Actually, I do know."

That was right. Gunnar knew the features of all the cities in Sofarende.

"But I don't think they're all still standing, so the one we came from is a good place to start. We know it's operating, at least."

We wandered until we saw the elevated train tracks, and we followed them to the station.

I had run out of the station so fast when we'd arrived, I hadn't bothered to look around. Or maybe they hadn't been there yet because it wasn't nighttime, but there were rows of people along the back wall with blankets, stretching out to sleep, or sitting up to talk to their neighbors.

Gunnar tried to direct me to the ticketing window to talk to someone, but I said, "Wait." He realized what I was doing and stopped walking.

I scanned every face.

"Nobody you know?"

I shook my head.

We continued to the ticket window.

"Hello," Gunnar said to the ticket man. "We were wondering if you might remember a family coming through here?"

"A mother, father, and two girls," I said.

He rubbed his forehead. "Do I remember a family?" He looked at our serious faces, then dropped the sarcasm from his voice. "I see a lot of people. I can't remember all of them. And I'm not the only person here. Did you check the board?"

"What board?"

"The message board. Used to be just a little thing, but you'll see, over there."

He pointed.

There was another long wall where no one was sleeping. It looked like there had once been an ordinary community bulletin board, but the messages had spilled out, tacked into the wall itself. Hundreds of them.

"Thank you," I said to the ticket man.

I ran over to the wall.

There were the kinds of things you might have expected on a bulletin board—missing cats, help wanteds—but then tacked over them were missing persons signs—my heart ached to see how many—and messages about how to find each other.

"Pickle": we went to Grandmother's.

Jacey and Tonna—if you need help, please look for us in Hillborg. Love from the Povels

Went to Gothen—the Boreps

Went to Kristiana—the Neels

Went to Skennel—the Sonnes

"There!" Gunnar cried, tapping one of the notices.

Went to Rothsted—the Josses

"Rothsted?" I asked. "I've never heard of it."

"'Rothsted,'" Gunnar recited, "'in the northeast of Sofarende. Has survived the war mainly intact. An agricultural rather than industrial town known for artisanal products such as breads and hand-embroidered cloths. No factories.'"

I threw my arms around him.

"How lucky am I to be traveling with a boy who knows every town in Sofarende?"

But Gunnar looked thoughtful.

"How come they didn't put your name on their note?"

"I don't think they were expecting me," I said.

"I would have been. When everything was over, wouldn't you come here?"

"Maybe they thought I would stay in Eilean."

Gunnar's mouth dropped open.

"What?" I asked.

"Our families didn't know we went to Eilean."

"I . . . I . . . oh." I looked at my shoes.

"You wrote to them?"

"No! No. Well, at the refugee camp, they let us send one postcard."

"So you *did* write to them."

"No, I just . . . addressed it . . . and put my handprint. I figured they would know it was me, and see the postmark. I was very careful. It would have meant nothing to anyone else. I promise."

He covered his face with his hands. "Mathilde . . ."

"I'm sorry! I—"

He put his hands down. "No, I suppose that was clever. I wished so many times I'd written to mine." He looked at the wall of messages again. He reached to take down the one from my family.

"Leave it." I pressed my hand to it. Father's writing. He'd touched this very paper the week before. "Maybe it's not addressed to me because it's for other people, too."

Gunnar pressed the tack back in.

"Do you see one from the Swillers? That's Megs's family."

We looked for a few more minutes.

"I don't think there is one," he said. "Come on. We have some train tickets to buy."

There wasn't going to be a train for us until the morning. We found a space against the wall in the rows of sleepers. Without blankets, it didn't feel right to lie down on the floor, so we just sat up against the wall.

Gunnar rummaged in his pack and took out some apples.

"Have two," he said, holding them out to me. "You need the water."

We ate, and then I rested my head on his chest to sleep.

Despite the two days of trains and buses, and walking through my ruined city, Gunnar smelled good.

"Thank you for helping me," I said.

His breathing deepened.

He was asleep.

Gunnar missed his family just as much as I missed mine. And he was willing to go all over Sofarende to find mine first, without complaining about it. He was willing to keep waiting.

I knew how hard that kind of waiting was.

I got up, trying very hard not to wake him, and walked back over to the ticket window.

31

A LOT OF PEOPLE waited on the train platform with us in the morning. So many wore rags. One woman had a chicken in a basket. While some people had company, many were traveling alone. But everyone seemed optimistic.

Going someplace, like the someplace could only be *better*.

"I got you a present." I reached into the lining of my sweater and fished out our tickets. "Here, this one's yours."

He stared at it.

Final destination: Holtzberg.

"But . . . when did you . . ."

I shrugged.

"Let me see yours."

Mine was the same as when he had bought it: Rothsted.

"We're supposed to stay together."

"I know, but . . . you said Rothsted is safe. I'll go there, I'll find my family, and everything will be fine. You need to know what's happened to your family. You need to go home."

He thought.

"We start on this train together?"

"Yes. You'll have to transfer later, but we'll start together. Then I stay on this one, all the way to Rothsted. It's perfect."

He bit his lip.

Then he smiled.

We managed to find two seats together. We ate whatever was left in our packs, which wasn't much. Train attendants came by once in a while with water, which we gulped out of tiny cups.

"How will we find each other again?" Gunnar asked.

"I'll leave a message in every train station I ever go to," I said.

"No, I mean, really, how will we find each other?"

I thought. "Why don't we write to Miss Markusen? We can ask where the other is. Things won't have to be so secret when the war is over."

"That's a good idea," he said. "It's strange. I had thought that once I was with my family again, I would be whole, and not be missing anyone. But it isn't true. When I think of our team, of all of us together, and how we probably won't be all together again, well ... there will always be someone to miss."

"I know exactly what you mean." The little threads in my heart reached for Megs again. Someday, I would have to tell her that when I went to our street, her house was gone. And that I didn't see her family's name on the message wall saying they were leaving town. I didn't know what had happened to them, and maybe we never would.

The train pulled into a large, crowded station. The station where Gunnar would transfer.

He put on his pack and hugged me tight.

"It will help with the missing," I said, "once we know that everyone is okay, wherever they are."

"I will still miss you anyway."

"Thank you for being my friend." I broke our hug. "Now go so you don't miss your train."

I watched through the window as Gunnar changed platforms. He picked a seat in a window where I could see him. His train pulled out first, and as we waved at each other, I hoped he couldn't see that I was crying.

My train didn't pull out. A lot more people boarded it. They packed in, sitting in every seat and even in the aisles. They stood when there wasn't any more room to sit.

"Why aren't we moving yet?" I asked the old woman who'd taken the seat next to me.

"Moving yet? We'll be lucky if we move today. This is only the second train going in this direction in weeks."

My heart started to pound and I suddenly felt hot.

"What do you mean?"

"They had to repair the tracks, they'd been hit. The first train went out this morning."

"So where have all the passengers been all that time? The ones who needed to go that way?"

"We've been here, at the station, in the town square."

Would my family have been held up here? Would they have changed their plans? Or would they be—on this train with me?

Mother, holding Tye's hand tight, helps her step onto the train. Tye is bouncing, excited, because she hasn't spent a lot of time on trains.

Kammi is calmer. She's worried about moving. About what

things will be like in their new home. About how long it will take them to find a house. About who she will play with. She keeps close to Father as they look for four seats on the crowded train.

"Dear?" the old woman said.

"Will you hold my seat, please?" I asked. "I'll be back in a few minutes."

"Of course," she said.

I picked my way through the people and luggage on the floor in the aisles. I looked into every compartment. I walked to the front of the train, then all the way through to the very last car. The door was still open, so I looked up and down the platform.

There weren't any more people waiting to board.

I made my way back to my seat.

They must have taken the train before us.

They must have.

We eventually started moving.

At first, my heart thrummed along with the sound of the train.

But as we traveled northward through the countryside, I began to feel a bit shaky. Like something was wrong.

That's just from the movement of the train. That's just because the train is shaky.

But when the attendant came to pass out small cups of water, the shakiness of the train didn't make anyone else in the compartment almost spill theirs. I was afraid to lift the cup to my lips, so I sat with it, setting the chipped white teacup against my leg.

"You should drink," the old woman next to me said. "They will be back to collect the cups soon, and who knows when there will be water again. With so many people, they might run out."

I nodded and sipped, but I could only sip a little. The water trickled into my empty stomach, reminding me how hungry I was. My stomach growled.

"You're all pink, dear," the old woman said. "Do you feel all right?"

A wobbliness in my stomach, a tightening in my chest.

"Something's wrong," I said.

"Maybe a trip to the washroom?" the woman asked kindly, keeping her voice low. But her voice faded out and back in, and the train's wheels went loud and soft, loud and soft, like someone was spinning the dial on a radio and picking up only snatches of the world around me.

"No, not like a trip to the washroom," I said. "More like . . . something went disconnected . . ." Or like I'd dropped something under the bed, but when I went to look for it, there was nothing there.

The old woman had a strange expression, like maybe she didn't know what to do for me. She patted my hand. "Try again to finish that water."

I swallowed it because I knew I needed water. But if the water made me sick, it would be better only to have had a little.

I needed help, but I didn't know what the help would be. Or I wanted *to* help, but I didn't know what needed to be done.

Maybe all it was, was being so close to ending the

waiting. Maybe, before it ended, it got so hard to wait that it nearly killed you.

The train stopped less frequently, passing through fields or forests for long stretches.

And then it stopped in the middle of nowhere.

I'd seen this happen before, but they didn't let anyone off, and they didn't pick anyone up.

"Why are we stopped?" I asked the old woman.

"I'm not sure. Maybe they're still working out repairs on the tracks?"

I peered out the window. It would be dark soon.

Then the train started going backward.

"Why are we going the wrong way?"

"Dear, I don't know any more than you do."

I looked at the people sitting across from me. "Why are we going backward?" My voice was shrill. They didn't answer.

We pulled into the last station we'd been through.

Conductors and Eilean and Sofarender soldiers started passing through all the cars.

"The route is impassable."

"Out of service."

"Service terminating here."

"Please leave the train."

"Please leave the train."

My head swam.

Why? What was wrong with the route?

I stumbled off the train in the sea of other passengers. I found an Eilean soldier and tugged his sleeve.

He looked surprised. I couldn't begin to explain that I was used to soldiers like him, that I had been to his country, that I had served, too. I had no papers on me anymore, and who would believe that story?

"What's going on?" I asked. Then I switched to Eilian. "What's *really* going on?"

He considered me. "The tracks were bombed."

"Bombed?" We were still bombing things? "By who?"

"Tyssians. We'd just fixed those tracks, but they didn't want the supply line open."

"What about—there was an earlier train that went out—"

"Hit."

"Hit?"

"There are crews out there, looking for survivors."

"Survivors? But that means—"

"Yes. There were victims."

My breath felt jagged and sharp entering my lungs. The black tunnel clouded my vision. But I had to stay on my feet, I had to explain . . . that disconnected feeling . . .

"Whoa." The soldier caught me, lightly slapped my face. "Stay with me. What is it?"

"I think . . . there may have been . . . people I knew on that train."

He walked me to a platform bench and helped me sit down. People streamed past, looking for somewhere to go. I didn't know how they had the energy to keep walking.

"Eat this." He handed me a candy.

The same kind of candy the soldiers at the camp had given me every day after I'd first arrived.

"I've missed these," I said.

He looked puzzled.

"I've—I've been to Eilean. Recently. The soldiers there gave me these, too."

"You've been to Eilean? I thought your Eilian sounded good. What in heaven did you come back here for?"

"To help. For the people on that train!"

"Sit, sit, sit," he said. "Eat that. I'll be right back."

I sucked on the candy, a sweet from another world. A safer, calmer world. Closing my eyes, I pretended I was just sitting outside with Micah. It didn't hurt to breathe anymore.

The soldier returned, with a conductor.

"He says you knew people on that train?" the conductor asked.

"I think, maybe."

"What makes you think that?"

"They were heading that way. And that was the only train. And I ... feel ... so ..."

"It's going to take them a while to sort out who was on that train. We don't know yet. Are you alone? Is there somewhere you can go to wait?"

"Yes. And I don't know. I don't think so. I have no idea where we are."

"There's a school that's been opened here, for people to stay in. You could go there for tonight, and we'll have a booth for information about the train's victims and survivors in the morning."

"Is the school like the camp? Will you sew numbers into my clothes?"

I started shaking. The two men looked at each other.

"Medical room, I think," the Eilean soldier said. "Come on, come with me, I'll walk you to the school."

The walk seemed long. The school was crowded, people staying in the hallways. They were probably the same people who'd had to be in the aisles on the train.

The soldier put his hand on my shoulder and steered me through the people to the door with a red mark on it. He spoke to the nurse, who had me sit, and then he spoke to the nurse some more. Then he left and the nurse came back to me.

In the nurse's room were several beds, most with people in them. She left me in my chair for a minute, and then brought me a steaming mug.

"Here, love, drink this."

I sipped the drink and grew sleepy within minutes. The nurse led me to a bed. Lying down was like a dream itself—in the past several days, I had only slept sitting up.

My mind went blank.

32

"WHAT IS THIS?" I asked, turning the yellow mush over with my spoon.

"Eggs," the morning nurse answered cheerfully. She seemed young, just a couple of years older than the Faetre kids.

I raised an eyebrow.

"Okay, they aren't *real* eggs. They're from a powder. But still, you should eat them. You need to eat something."

I set my spoon down.

"Juice?" she offered.

"Is it—"

"Real juice? Well, no. But it has some vitamins in it."

I sipped the "juice." It was orangey. Sort of.

The nurse sat down on the end of my bed.

"I'm supposed to tell you, when you feel up to it, that there's a table at the town hall for information about passengers on that train."

My stomach churned. I handed her my plate of pretend eggs.

"Juice," the nurse directed. "You aren't going anywhere until you drink that."

• • •

When she let me leave, I was surprised to find that it was already afternoon. I'd been asleep for hours. How could I have wasted all that time sleeping?

The town hall was easy to find, not too far from the school. I asked in the front where I could find out about the train.

I approached the right table, where a woman sat with clipboards of lists.

"I'm here about the train."

"Yes," she said. "What name are you looking for?"

"The family name is Joss," I said.

She went through her lists, running her pencil down the columns.

Her pencil stopped.

"I'm sorry to tell you this, dear. I do have some Josses. Three. On the list of the deceased."

The pretend juice came roaring back up. It spattered all over the woman's table and all over her terrible lists.

I had known. I had known since it had happened. Somehow. I had felt them go out of this world.

"I'm afraid you're very ill," the woman was saying. She sounded far away, but she was pushing me into a chair. I let her bend my body to do it; I wasn't in control anymore. I coughed up the rest of the juice onto her dusty floor.

When everything stopped spinning, I picked up my head.

The woman was still standing there, looking alarmed.

"Wait," I managed to say.

She waited.

"Did you say you only had three?"

33

THE LARGE ROOM HAD maybe eighty cots in rows.

Not unlike the family room at the camp. But smaller. Without the grown-ups.

Clusters of girls played clapping games and boys pushed each other around. Wherever they sent us kids, there was always tag. Always.

On every cot: simple stuffed bears or elephants or tigers or cloth dollies.

Someone had thought of these children and given each a lovey?

A lovey couldn't replace what was gone from them, of course. But it was a nice thought all the same.

No one had given me a lovey in a long time.

It had taken the grown-ups days just to track this place down for me. To confirm that it was where I should go.

This place, one of many, for the war's unclaimed children.

Most of the children were noisy and playing. My eyes scanned them.

. . .

She sat alone, as if frozen on the edge of her bed, her blond hair pulled into tight braids.

The way Mother had always done them.

But Mother hadn't done them this time.

Mine, neither.

Never would again.

I walked to her as if drawn there by a magnet. I stood in front of her.

"Kammi?"

She looked up, but like she didn't know it was me.

"Oh, Kammi . . ."

I pressed her head against my chest and held her and held her. But she stayed stiff.

"It's me," I said. "It's Mathilde."

I let her go and looked into her face again. Could she have forgotten me?

Even sitting down, she looked taller than I remembered. Because it had been what, almost a year? Ten lifetimes? Her face looked thinner and her eyes were sunken into dark, greenish circles.

"I've come to take you home," I said.

She lowered her eyes and started twisting the skirt of her dress. Then she set her hands on the bed and stayed absolutely still.

"We don't have a home."

"Come on," I said.

But where are we going?

"Do you have . . . things?"

She blinked at me.

Right.

I didn't have things, either. I'd left my pack behind some-where, probably on the train.

"Well, here, let's bring this." I picked up the cloth dolly from her bed. It had a blue patchwork dress and blue stitched eyes.

Why?

"Someone gave it to you, that was nice."

It was good to think there were still some people who were nice.

I held the dolly out to her, and she took it, held it to her chest like someone had told her that was what you were sup-posed to do with dolls.

Tye, she would have forgotten everything bad, and been happy to have this doll. She would have run and played with the other children, she would have . . .

I closed my eyes against the throw-up feeling rising in my throat.

Kammi was still alive, in front of me.

Had she seen them broken, after?

"Kammi, Kammi," I said, opening my eyes as both pain and relief swelled in my chest. "Kammi, it really is me. I'm still here. And we're leaving now, together. Come on."

She wouldn't look me in the eyes.

Where are we going?

I sat down next to her.

I closed my eyes again.

Pictured home.

Mother making dinner. The smell of roasting meat and veg-etables, like there'd been no trouble at the market.

Father arriving from work, taking off his coat and cap, hugging me and Kammi and Tye. Big, Middle, Little.

Would Kammi still be Middle, even though there was nobody to be between?

I was still Big.

Still going to take care of my sister.

I closed my eyes to picture home again.

Something else came to mind. Something I hadn't expected.

Glowing like a bright hope.

Like the blue world Rainer and I had imagined. Where people took care of each other. Where people were kind, even to strangers.

Especially to strangers.

I'd been left with this one piece of my first home, my first family, and that was Kammi. I pressed my hand over hers, even though she flinched, and held tight.

But out there, there was another piece, if I could find it, and claim it back.

If I fought for it.

I closed my eyes. I reached within myself to pick up the scattered pieces, the threads. To hold tight and let them guide me.

I tugged Kammi's hand.

"Come on."

I stood, tried to pull her up with me, but she resisted.

"We're not . . . going to take the train, are we?"

"No," I promised. "No more trains."

34

WE WALKED.

We walked, and slept in barns, and town squares.

We walked, and I stole two coats from an empty house.

We walked, and ate acorns from the woods.

We walked, and washed in streams, and I braided our hair tight.

We walked, and in a random town, on a random day, with people we'd never met before, we heard the news that Sofarende, every inch of her, was free.

We walked, and, one day, Kammi smiled.

We walked as far as we could walk, and then we stopped, and looked out across the sea.

35

THE GENTLE RISE AND fall of the waves caressed me and settled me down on the sand, where I slept soundly. For a long time, until the wind woke me.

There down the beach was Father.

He came into sight, flickering like always.

The flicker echoed as fear in my heart, because I knew that next the wind would dissolve his image altogether.

He would go, as he always did.

But the beach was calm, with a brilliant blue sky above and white foaming waves, and my fear was extinguished.

His image stayed.

Grew clearer.

He waved.

I looked down at my own hand, squeezed and released my fist easily. Held it up in front of me.

I waved back.

"Big!" he called.

I stood up and walked to him.

He wasn't disappearing. He wasn't blinking in and out of sight.

There was no hurry, so I walked slowly, at first feeling the sand beneath my feet, and then, nothing beneath my feet at all.

I reached him.

"Father."

"Big."

His arms wrapped around me, and I could feel them, for a moment, but as I settled into our hug, the feeling of his arms faded, like the sensation of the sand beneath my feet had quickly been forgotten.

But he wasn't gone from me. I knew he was still there.

I could see him, bright bright bright.

I met his eyes.

"You've done well, Big."

"I tried. I'm still trying."

"I'm sorry we couldn't have more time together. But I'm not sorry I sent you away. You survived. And you are there for Kammi."

"Is Tye with you?"

"Our Little is with us, yes." The skin around his eyes wrinkled. He looked so, so sad, but also, somehow, at peace.

A chill swept over my toes, my ankles, wet but soothing.

I looked down; a wave was receding, sucking the sand out from under my feet and rushing back toward the sea while another gathered itself to meet me.

The waves *were* lapping my feet.

"Kammi!" I cried. "Kammi, get up! The tide's coming in!"

Kammi woke quickly, realized where she was, and bounded up the beach, shrieking.

I followed behind and met her to sit on some rocks to catch our breath.

"Maybe sleeping on the beach was a bad idea," she said.

"Sorry," I said.

But then Kammi was laughing. I put my arm around her.

The beach had been so nice at night. I'd wanted to look at the stars.

The morning light hid them, of course, but they were still there.

Things that are far away can still guide you.

With them out of sight of my eyes, I fixed my heart on them.

Then I looked at Kammi, who was, by a miracle and my own effort, with me.

Before, I had never thought about how Kammi looked like our parents. But suddenly, I could see it. When she worried, her brow creased, just like Mother's. If she smiled, it was Father's smile.

You are from your mother, so she's always with you.

Mother would always be with us.

And Father, too.

36

"WHY WOULD HE TAKE us?" Kammi asked.

"Because we're going to pay him to."

I pulled every last orin out of my sweater.

Kammi's eyes went wide.

I marched down the pier to the ferryman.

Free entry into Eilean hadn't been established yet. But there were a few channels opening again. For some people.

"I want to go across," I said. "Me and my sister."

"You might be turned right around," he said.

"I won't be. I have the documents all ready on the Eilean side. There are people waiting for me. I'll pay you. Half up front, and half when we get there."

"How much?"

I showed him.

Everything I had.

I wouldn't need the orins anymore.

"Deal."

• • •

In Eilean, soldiers detained us in a port office, but after a few hours and a few telephone calls, we were issued new entry papers.

I paid the ferryman, as I had promised. It felt right that the money the Examiner had given Father for my military service, and then Father had given to me, would have paid our passage. Like the two of them had thought of everything.

And I had done everything I could to be worthy of it.

"Someone will be around to collect you," the clerk told us.

We sat on a bench in the front hall, swinging our feet.

If they collected us, we would be taken to the aerial center.

But I wanted to go somewhere else.

None of the adults were watching.

"Come on," I said to Kammi. I offered her my hand.

"Are they here?" she asked, when there was no one for us outside.

"Not yet," I said.

We came to the gate. I showed our papers. We went through.

It was easy.

Then we had to walk again.

We walked along the coastline.

To 510 Sealane.

No one was outside.

We walked up onto the porch.

I touched the three poppies. Knocked. Knocked again. Then put my hands on Kammi's shoulders.

Mr. Parmeter opened the door. His mouth fell open when he saw me, but then his arms did, too, and he lifted me up and held me against him like I was small, arms around my back and letting my feet dangle.

"I've worried about you since the day I dropped you off. Never was sure I did the right thing."

"You did," I said as he set me down. I touched Kammi's shoulders again. "This is my sister, Kammi."

"Your sister?"

"Yes. I picked her up in Sofarende."

"You ... picked her up?" Mr. Parmeter looked like he wanted to sit down. You didn't just swing by a war-torn country to pick people up.

"Kammi? Could you sit on the step?"

She scrunched her nose. She didn't like secrets. But she went to sit, and I led Mr. Parmeter farther down the porch.

"We've been walking for weeks. I need to go to the aerial intelligence center, but I don't want her to see the aerials and the guns. She's seen enough. Can she stay here, and rest, and eat? She won't be any trouble. I'll come back."

"Of course. Whatever you need."

I knelt in front of Kammi and looked up into her face.

She set her mouth in a frown.

"Please, Kammi, we've all had to be brave. It's just one little thing more. The last thing. And then we'll be together."

Finally she whispered, "You left before."

"That was different. That was for a long time. This is for just a short time. I promise."

She looked unconvinced.

I bit my lip. I'd made and broken that promise before.

I would have to do much better this time.

"They have a girl about your age," I said. "She's really nice."

"I'll get her right now," Mr. Parmeter said. He disappeared, and returned with Angelica.

Angelica threw her arms around me. "You came back."

"Course I did. Angelica, will you take care of my sister? I'll be back as soon as I can."

Angelica's eyes went wide as she took in Kammi. "Dada?" she asked.

"Same as before," he said. "Food. Water. Bath. Sleep." Then he looked at me. "You, too."

"I can't. I have to go."

"Then I'll drive you," Mr. Parmeter said.

Angelica extended a hand to Kammi. She didn't take it. But she stepped closer to the doorway, toward the warmth and the light. Toward the real house. Toward a meal and a bath.

I handed Mr. Parmeter some documents.

"Her name's Kammi. These are her papers. In case you need them."

He took them. "Don't worry. She'll be safe here." He disappeared for a minute to put the papers inside and came back with some bread for me. "Now, explain again where you need to go."

"I have to ask," Mr. Parmeter said, once we'd been on the road for a while. "Your family . . ."

My throat felt all closed up.

"If you brought your sister here, does that mean . . . ?"

I nodded. "We're . . . we're the only ones left."

I kept my eyes ahead as we drove.

I saw a vision of a girl in navy on a bicycle.

"Stop!" I yelled to Mr. Parmeter, opening my door and jumping out as soon as he'd slowed enough.

She came closer and closer.

Where was she going?

She braked the bicycle right in front of me.

"What are you doing?" she asked.

"What are *you* doing?"

She looked embarrassed. "I'm out for a bicycle ride."

"Because . . . ?"

"Because I wanted to go for a bicycle ride?"

"Really?"

"No. Because we'd heard you'd landed but we didn't know *where* you were. Again, Mathilde?"

But then she grinned, and I hugged her.

We figured out how to get her bicycle into the backseat and she climbed into the front with me.

"How is everyone?" I asked.

"Good!"

We passed the refugee center.

Which looked like it had fewer people within the fences.

"How about them?" I asked. "Do you know anything?"

"Your friend Micah left," Annevi said.

"He did?"

"Yeah. He and his family got released."

"Do you know where they went?"

"When Sofarende opened again, they were going to try to go home."

"Oh," I said, disappointed that I couldn't see him. But really, I was glad for him.

"Some of the other kids, the ones without family, went to Eilean families."

"That's good," I said.

And as we neared the aerial intelligence station, the gladness filled me.

I hoped very much that Micah's home was still there.

And wished myself luck as I went to collect what was left of mine.

When we got to the station, Annevi went to find the Examiner, who met me and Mr. Parmeter at his car, outside the gates.

I ran to her. She beamed and hugged me. She held me for a long time and stroked my hair.

"Gunnar?" I asked.

"He wrote. He and his family are fine."

"And Rainer?"

"We think he's safe, too."

"And . . . ?"

"Room four-oh-six. Go!"

"Thank you!"

I ran, leaving the Examiner and Mr. Parmeter talking.

Megs was alone, with charts and papers scattered all over a table. She looked up as I crossed the room and sat down in the chair opposite her.

I smiled.

The corners of her mouth turned up, just a little.

"I made it," I said.

"Yes," she said.

Then we were quiet, looking at each other. Time rolled backward in my mind, replacing Megs's short hair with the braids we'd grown up with. The purple fatigue under her eyes with rosy cheeks. Her blue eyes, though, those were the same as they always had been. Welcoming and trusting.

But her face also said she didn't want to be trusting.

Trusting could get you hurt.

People you loved could just disappear.

People you loved could hurt you.

My smile faded.

I had terrible things to tell her. About her house. And not seeing a note from her family on the train station message board.

"I'm sorry I didn't stay with you. The night we left Faetre. I'm not sorry about what I did instead. I'm sorry that it made you not want to be friends anymore."

She sighed. "I know that was something you had to do."

"Then why do you hate me so much?"

She picked up her pencil as if to mark something very important on her map. "I don't hate you."

"Then what's the matter?"

"I'm ..." She flipped the pencil, erased the lines she'd just drawn. Erased and erased so it looked as if they'd never been there. "I was ... afraid."

"Of me? Why?"

She marked regions all over Sofarende, shaded some in. "What does it look like? Sofarende, I mean."

"What?" It would have been a random question if not for

the map in front of her. "Oh . . . well, it looks awful. For the most part." I took a deep breath. "Our street . . . it's mostly gone. The . . . the people, too."

She swallowed hard. Drew several buildings. Then she scribbled them out and threw the pencil at the wall.

"It wasn't just about me and Rainer, then, was it?"

Megs shook her head. Buried her face in her hands. Then she was shaking. Crying.

"Megs?" I put an arm on her elbow. She didn't pull away.

She, like me, had had to make decisions.

She had had to believe, by choice, that she was doing the right thing. Knowing that there was a lot of room to be wrong.

"Megs?"

"There were also things that *I* had to do."

"I know."

"And you make me talk about things. *Think* about things. I didn't want to talk. I didn't want to think." She finally met my eyes. "I'm really not going back to Sofarende. I can't see it. Not like that."

"I know."

She had hurt it to save it. She was afraid to see what she had done.

That would always be a part of her.

The war would always be a part of her.

An ugly part, for all the triumph of having won. For having helped the best she could.

For years we had known each other better than anyone else.

And maybe we still did.

"I love you," I said. Saying it was easy. True. "I came to get you. Come with me."

"I'm not going back, I told you."

"I know. I have somewhere else for us to go. I'm on leave—maybe you could be, too. They won't need as many of us now. They had said we could go when the war was over. And isn't it? We'll ask the Examiner. She owes us, I think."

I remembered when she'd brought me Megs at Faetre, when I was at my lowest, when I'd no longer felt like myself.

Wouldn't she want to help Megs now?

Wasn't that why she'd sent me right up?

I took Megs's hand, and went to find the Examiner.

37

THE NEXT DAY, HAMLIN fitted short, thick bars on either side of my bicycle's back tire.

Megs stood on the bars as I pushed off, hands on my shoulders, extra civilian clothes in a pack on her back.

No more uniforms.

We each risked letting go with one hand to wave back at Hamlin and Tommy, the other boys, Annevi . . . Miss Markusen. Especially Miss Markusen.

I had a small card she'd given me in my pocket, with just a few lines: Gunnar's address. I could write to him, as much as I wanted, because the war was over. No more rules about letters.

I didn't know how long Megs looked back at everyone, but I had to concentrate on moving us forward. Megs's weight on the bicycle was nothing extra; I felt lighter, somehow, with her along.

The sea shone as we coasted along the roads. Sometimes, when the light changed, we could see Sofarende.

We picked up speed down the hills; we had to lean

into the curves. But Megs never tightened her grip on my shoulders.

She trusted me.

It was still light out when we finally got there.

Kammi, as if she had been waiting at the window for the past two days, rushed out of the house.

Scrubbed clean, hair tightly braided.

She ran and hugged me and Megs at once, hitting us hard as she threw her arms around us.

Megs closed her eyes and held my sister. "Kammi . . . when I heard . . . I'm so glad you're okay. . . ."

Angelica toppled into our hug. "You're all staying!"

Angelica's mother came onto the porch, drying her hands on her apron. Angelica's dada followed.

He'd arranged everything with Miss Markusen.

I smiled as he caught my eye, but it was a wobbly smile. The kind that happens before you cry.

As our hug broke apart and the other girls went inside ahead of me, Angelica gabbing to Megs, I held back. I was last to the porch, where the only one left was Angelica's dada.

"Thank you."

He hugged me.

He knelt, took my hands.

"None of this was your fault. If I can give you girls some safety here, I want to. I hope that, in your country, someone was kind to my boys."

"I'm sorry about your sons." I met his eyes. Didn't look away.

He hugged me again. It wasn't like when Father used to

200

hug me, and never would be, but I relaxed, glad for it all the same.

Inside, Angelica and Kammi were excited to show me and Megs our room.

It had been the boys' room. Slanted ceilings, gabled windows facing the sea and Sofarende, and three beds.

All three beds were made up. One had Kammi's lovey doll on it.

On another, under the slanted ceiling like where I'd always slept at home back in Lykkelig, was a folded piece of clothing.

I walked over slowly and picked it up.

My nightgown, clean and white again, all stains removed.

The rips and tears had been mended with careful, neat stitches of an almost-white, but just slightly blue, thread that ran in gentle rivers all over the bottom of the skirt. Where the rips had been larger, patches of shiny white were held in place by the blue stitches.

Perhaps she had been out of white thread and couldn't get more, but it looked beautiful this way.

We couldn't hide or cover up what the cloth had been through; we had to accept that it had been patched back together and would be forever a little bit different.

I hugged it. I would have to tell Angelica's mother how much I loved it.

I would wear it, sleep for a million and a half years with only good dreams, and then, in the morning, I would wake up and start a new day.

I reached into my bag and carefully pulled out the paintings.

They'd hung on walls. Been carried out of Sofarende. Soaked in the sea. Locked in a safe. Shut in a drawer.

Had survived, mostly intact.

On the slanted ceiling across from the pillow that would be my pillow, I pinned up our handprints. Big, Middle, Little.

Kammi gasped.

"You still have that?"

"Of course I do."

She walked over and pressed her left hand over the middle-sized left hand.

"I grew," she said.

"Good," I said.

Then she moved her hand to cover Tye's left handprint in the center of the paper.

Tye would never grow.

Would never press her hand to this paper to see how much bigger she was.

Would never hold our hands again.

We had brought only this small piece of her out of Sofarende.

That, and the pieces we carried in our hearts, stitched in so carefully that she would be there always.

Kammi kept her hand pressed over Tye's print. She was crying. I wrapped myself around her and rocked her as I cried, too.

Later, I opened the other painting and pinned up Rainer's blue world.

The Parmeter family was the closest I'd come to seeing it since the war began.

They could have been shut off and angry about what they'd lost.

But when I'd climbed out of the sea, a stranger, they'd welcomed me.

And they were giving us a home, somewhere to feel safe. "Girls! Dinner!"

Angelica and Kammi ran off.

But Megs stayed with me.

"You'll like it here," I said.

"If you're here, that's enough for me."

I smiled at her but glanced at the painting again.

"Do you know where Rainer is?" she asked.

"No," I said. "I hope he's all right."

"Me too," she said. "I mean it."

"I know you do."

Whatever happens, I'll be with you.

She'd made me that promise long ago.

And in turn, we'd both broken it, in one way or another.

But we could begin again.

We could stand together as we built our new world. We looked at the picture for another minute; then Megs held out her hand. "Dinner?"

"Of course," I said, and slipped my hand in hers.

THE STORY BEGINS IN

Beautiful Blue World

SUZANNE LaFLEUR

CITIZENS OF SOFARENDE:

Due to the continued conflict with Tyssia, please be advised of new mandatory safety instructions.

Be on alert at all times for the sirens.

At the sound of the sirens, proceed immediately to your assigned shelter. Do not leave your shelter for any reason. Remain there until the all-clear siren sounds.

Shelter assignment:

Residence: Joss, 52 Raken Street, Lykkelig

Shelter: Heller, basement level, 54 Raken Street, Lykkelig

1

MEGS AND I FROZE on my front step.

We'd seen the notices on our walk home, pinned to every door, fluttering in the chill winter breeze: white butterflies tacked down, wishing to fly free.

It was better to think of them that way, like butterflies.

Because they also looked like white flags of surrender.

"Did you get one?" I asked, craning my neck to check two doors down, where Megs lived.

"Everyone did."

I looked at her, my best friend and opposite-twin, her dark braids mirroring my light ones. She realized the edge in her tone. It had snuck in, at least once a day, since her father had left to fight. Been ordered to fight.

It's not you she's mad at.

Her bright blue eyes, watering in the cold, took me in. A smile came to them as one appeared across her pink, chapped cheeks. "Come on, let's see what mine says." She offered her hand, led me past the Hellers' between us, to her own house. "See, we're assigned together! Whatever it is, it won't be so bad, Mathilde."

"But—why do we need shelter assignments?"

Mother, waiting for me to get home, opened our front door. She saw me and smiled, lifted her hand to wave. But then she spotted the notices across the street and turned to read ours. She grew very still; her smile disappeared.

Mrs. Heller opened her door, too. She read her notice, looked around at all of us. Her face swelled like a boiled red potato.

"Now you're going to be living at my house?"

"Living? How long do you expect us to be down there?" Mother asked.

"Who knows? Maybe forever. But your family's not to become a burden on our family; you'd better send over some food stores—"

"Food stores? I'm not sending my food stores over to your basement. You'll eat them!"

"Are you accusing me of being a thief?"

"That's what you've implied I am!"

My little sisters came to the doorway: Kammi, who had beaten me home from school, and Tye, blouse untucked and short braids falling out. I raced home, Megs at my heels. "Come on," I said to my sisters. "Come inside."

I quickly shut the door. The house was cold. There wasn't enough fuel for fires during the day anymore.

"Here, Tye, let's find your sweater." A sweater that had once been mine, and then Kammi's, and now had patches on the elbows.

"Catch me!" Tye shrieked.

She didn't need to know that I felt wobbly, that we might be headed to live in the basement next door. I chased her into the living room, grabbed her by the ankles, and held her upside down.

"I'm upside down! I'm upside down!" She giggled.

Poor Tye had never known the world right-side up. Before Tyssia decided they wanted all of it for themselves; before they took over the Skaven lands, before they joined with Erobern.

Before they were coming for us.

Mother came in and slammed the door. I dropped Tye, who rolled away, laughing.

"Why are we going to the Hellers' basement?" I asked Mother.

"Ours is too shallow."

"Too shallow for what?"

I followed her into the kitchen, where she loaded up a box with tins and jars. There hadn't been that much in the pantry to begin with. *Don't grumble, don't grumble,* I told my stomach as the shelves emptied.

Mother handed me the heavy box, adjusting the red scarf around my neck and freeing my braids. "Take this next door."

Was she afraid, like Mrs. Heller, that we were going to have to *live* in their basement?

For how long?

Forever?

I looked at Megs, who shrugged.

"Why don't you do your homework at Megs's house?" Mother said.

"Why is she mad at you? You didn't ask the government to send those notices."

And wouldn't Mrs. Heller want to help us, if there was some kind of emergency? She was our neighbor. Kammi played with her daughter.

Mother smiled, grazed her knuckle down my cheek. "Don't you worry. Run along."

Megs and I walked to the Hellers' in silence. Megs knocked. When Mrs. Heller answered, she looked less like a boiled potato, but she took our box with a huff and slammed the door.

"It's probably like a drill," Megs said as we walked to her house. "Like fire drills at school. We practice those all the time, and have we ever had a fire? No. We'll probably never have to go to her stupid basement."

She ripped down her family's notice on the way through the door. She stopped to look me in the eye.

"Even if we do, we'll be together. Whatever happens, I'll be with you."

ABOUT THE AUTHOR

Suzanne LaFleur is the author *of Love, Aubrey; Eight Keys; Listening for Lucca;* and *Beautiful Blue World.* She lives in New York City, where she decorates her walls with the handprints of children she loves. Visit her online at suzannelafleur.com.